You Can Have It
When I'm Through
with It

Betty Webb Mace

You Can Have It When I'm Through with It

DAUGHTERS, INC.

Plainfield, Vermont

To my three Muses:

Verla,
Lavada,
and Mary Rose

You Can Have It
When I'm Through
with It

Opening the medicine cabinet and finding one lonely
can of Chef-Boy-Ar-Dee Spaghetti-Os, Jenny West decided that she had come to the end of the proverbial
road. Starvation lurked. She was cold, too. Although
the Los Angeles Chamber of Commerce was still bab-
bling about the balmy Southern California weather,
Jenny had found February in Tinsel Town somewhat
less than tropic. She pulled her army blanket tighter
and sniffed despondently.

The studio window framed a dismal scene. Outside, the skies had opened like flushed toilets and dirty
brown water stood ankle deep in the streets. "Like hell
it never rains in California," she muttered to herself.
"Just in October, November, December, January, February, March, and April." She paused for a moment,
picked a flake of paint off her wrist with a broken fin-
gernail, and added, "Piss. Piss on this whole state." She
wiped her nose with a dirty hand.

Los Angeles didn't seem to be working out for her.
Even after a residency of eight years, her midwestern
pragmatism still stood in rebellion against the conceits
of coastal life. Where Midwesterners would sensibly install storm drains, Californians denied that the rain ex-
isted and splashed through drenched, drainless streets.

She sniffed again, set the can of Spaghetti-Os on her
hot plate, then crumbled a One-A-Day vitamin pill and
a protein wafer on top of the spaghetti. She stirred the
mixture with a plastic spoon and while humming the
"Artist's Life" waltz, waited for her lunch to boil.

Fleetingly, she wondered if Carlos might be per-
suaded to install a heating system in the studio but as
soon as the idea appeared, she dismissed it with a grin.

Not Carlos Cornejo, the Tenants' Trial.

"Ah, Mees West," he whined when collecting the rent. "The life of a lonlord is so sod. No money. Only troubles."

He was careful, Jenny noted, to park his Mercedes at a safe distance from the studio and to turn his ring so that the large diamond nestled discreetly against his soft palm.

"Erbody treat poor Chicano so bod. Take advantages. Be late with rents. My poor Rosita, she make her own tortillas, her work so, so hard. 'Get the rents,' she cries to me, her hons so red from the works she do. 'Get the rents, Carlos!' So here I am, me with the heart of gold— but what can thees poor mon do?"

Then he would stuff the rent into the pocket of his cashmere suit.

In the four years that Jenny had lived in the studio, he had not yet come through with the promised furniture and so the place was as devoid of comfort as a bus stop restroom.

The studio measured fifteen by twenty feet, not large by studio standards, but adequate. The walls were covered with crumbling stucco and at the far end was a three-foot-high graffiti entitled "Jesus Sucks." Jenny attributed this esoteric bit of information to the former tenant—a satanist who was now languishing in jail for the ceremonial beheading of a kidnapped Lhasha Apso.

There was no furniture other than a small, uncovered mattress, an easel, and a tipsy, three-legged stool. Jenny knew from experience that the more comfortable she was, the less painting she did. If she had a couch she would sit on it. All day. And if blessed with a bed she would soon fall into the habit of taking four-hour naps twice daily. Given a television she would watch "Love of Life," "Hollywood Squares," "Gilligan's Island," "Mike Douglas," "Hee Haw," "Ironside," and finish up

4

the day with "Sermonette."

She ate her meal in silence, listening to the Niagara outside. When she finished, she wiped the spoon off with a paint rag and tossed the paper plate into the corner. Her housework thus completed, she sat down on the mattress and began to think.

She had two dollars left and after visiting the laundromat that evening, there would be nothing. The advertising agency she had been doing free-lance illustrations for had changed to photography, leaving her with no income at all. There appeared no prospects of income for a full two months—when her one-woman show would be opening at the Pearce Gallery.

On her fingers Jenny tried to count off her marketable skills, but being a true child of the twentieth century, she didn't get past her thumb. In growing despair, she realized that besides painting she couldn't do a thing. She couldn't type, keep books, clean a house, lube a car, lance a boil, or sweep a street. The usual stand-by of prostitution was open to her, but it was Jenny's conceit that she was too fastidious. In more lucid moments she would admit that this wasn't true—the twentieth century having crept also between her thighs. But desperate women held on to their illusions.

What to do? What to do?

She regarded the unfinished painting that was secured on the easel. It was a five-by-eight oil in shades of grays and browns, portraying a circle dance performed by six emaciated corpses. *Danse Macabre* she called it—the story of her life. Turning from *Danse Macabre,* she looked at the drying oils on the south studio wall, so large in contrast to the acrylic on the east wall. Jenny preferred working with acrylics because of the medium's quick-drying properties and their relative immunity to accident. She still agonized over the night she had rolled drunk and naked off her mattress against a wet oil, imprinting a shadowy scene on her backside.

The paintings stared accusingly at her. They needed frames for which she had no money. *Danse Macabre* needed some yellow ochre. The bottle of linseed oil was down to a scant quarter-inch in depth and her last dab of glazing gel had long since dried into a hard gray marble. With a sigh more of resignation than despair, Jenny rolled up her frayed sleeves and began to paint.

Four hours later Jenny decided to stop for the day. It was getting dark and she was starved. She began the ritual of cleaning up, first covering the unused paint on her palette with Saran Wrap so it wouldn't dry out. This accomplished, and the palette set safely on the window ledge, she slowly and methodically cleaned the brushes. She swished them through pure, clean turpentine and then washed them in warm, soapy water—first testing the water carefully on her wrist. If too hot, the water could melt the glue which held the bristles together—a financial disaster since good sable brushes cost anywhere from two dollars to fifteen dollars apiece. After making sure the caps were twisted tightly on the bright tubes of paint she finally began the more unpleasant job of cleaning herself up.

She rubbed turpentine onto her paint-splattered skin. It burned and she knew she would have a rash for several hours. Then she tried her best to wash away the pungent smell. She was only mildly successful. Her best friends had told her that she did not smell like a flower—that she smelled more like the assembly line at Hughes Aircraft.

Discarding her mechanic's overalls, she put on her last clean shirt and slipped into a pair of Levis that had only been worn four times since being washed. No underwear. Her last pair of underpants had fallen apart in the washer some three months back. She hadn't worn a bra in years. The natural look, she thought grimly.

She began to gather up her dirty clothes—three pairs of faded Levis, five shirts, and one dirty pair of U. S. Keds. Stuffing them into a plastic garbage bag, she steeled herself for the six-block-walk through the California liquid sunshine.

As she splashed up the street she consoled herself with visions of her ex-classmates in cooler climes. They had gone on to brilliant art directorships in prestige agencies but were freezing (she hoped) their hip suede-covered butts off.

This section of Beverly Boulevard was typically schizophrenic. It was lined with topless beer bars (Come On In! 4 Koy Kittens!), drug crisis centers, clever boutiques, and a few stucco homes sitting back, horrified, behind their hurricane fences.

Peering through the rain (at least it dissolved the smog), she managed a damp smile. Los Angeles architecture never failed to amuse her. Office buildings and car washes modeled after pagan temples, then painted cherry pink, pistachio green, lemon yellow, and blueberry blue.

Protected only slightly by a leaky plastic umbrella she had found discarded in a garbage can, she hurried down the street towards the Straights and Swingers apartments. That complex, a massive thousand-unit beehive for singles, had become a blessing to the other denizens of the neighborhood. They could wash for twenty-five cents in one of the daisy yellow washers and then dry for free. The managers were always trying to catch these bootleg users, but as yet had devised no successful method of keeping them out. Their scheme of locking the laundry room and supplying only bona fide

7

lease holders with keys had backfired. Two bombs had been set off—one blasting down the locked door, the other melting all the plastic plants in the building's chandeliered entrance. After that, the locks came off.

Besides being cheap, the laundry room had all the comforts of home. There was a fully stocked library containing back issues of *Playboy* (minus centerfolds). *Cosmopolitan* (minus centerfolds), *Argosy*, Gothic paperbacks, *The Daily Worker*, and *Dune Buggy Quarterly*. The walls were lined with vending machines dispensing everything from Chanel No. 5 to parsleyed chicken soup. One day, Jenny thought, some enterprising soul would roll a bed down there and another aspect of the Good Life could be taken care of while the wash went round and round.

She arrived at the Straights and Swingers slightly damp and noticed to her relief that the laundry room was less crowded than usual. Apparently few of the bootleggers had cared to brave the rain. Hot house roses, those Californians. Humming "Walking in the Rain," she dumped all of her things into one washer; the time was long gone when she cared about fading.

At the vending machines she bought a Scooter Pie and a cup of soup, and then sat sighing in one of the vinyl chairs. The air was warm and humid, stiff with the smell of detergent and bleach. She looked around. On a bench against the wall sat the Swinging Single men, all looking chagrined over the fact that nobody loved them enough to do their laundry for them. A social stigma. The Swinging Single women, hair combed and dressed, chatted brightly in front of the men, folding their washing in neat piles—hoping that the men would notice how domestic, how pleasant they were. How available.

Business as usual, Jenny thought. Everybody on the make. She herself was being looked at like a marked-down sirloin strip at Safeway. The air crackled with imminent come-here-oftens and wet-enough-for-yas.

Shuddering, she picked up a copy of the *Woman's Companion* and scanned the articles. "Rape. It Could Happen to You." "How to Make Perfect Creamed Chipped Beef Every Time." "God Heard My Prayers and Gave Me Little Cindy." (That one turned out to be about a retarded child. A dirty trick, God.) Depressed, she tried the "Letters to the Editor."

Dear Companion,

My husband was killed in Viet Nam, leaving me with eight children—one crippled with cerebral palsy, two blind, and four mentally retarded. My house burned down and we lost our cocker spaniel. My children and I are now living in a two-room house right under the freeway off-ramp, only half a block from the rendering plant. Still, I thank God for making me a woman and finding me worthy enough to test my faith.

A Christian Mother

Dear Companion,

My little boy (age seven) came home from school the other day and said to me, "Mommy, are you and Daddy really married or just living together?" Shocked, I asked him *what* he meant and he said, "The only kids in my class whose parents aren't divorced are the ones who never got married in the first place."

Well, Companion. I tell you! Things are coming to a pretty pass in this great nation of ours if a little boy has to ask a question like *that*! If men have gotten so that they can't do the right thing by a woman (all my husbands did with me) then I just don't know what's going to happen. It's all the fault of that sick Women's Liberation movement.

Shocked in Des Moines

Dear Companion,

Did you know that if you save the red plastic strip from cigarette packages you can help a blind man get a seeing-eye dog? I always remember that when I light up.

An Unselfish Smoker

9

Dear Companion,

In case some of your readers out there were wondering what to do with all of those empty egg cartons, here's a tip!

Staple four of them together (after removing the lids) and spray them with metallic gold or silver paint. The finished product can be hung on the wall for a delightful bit of whimsy.

Creative Housewife

Sorry, creative housewife, thought Jenny. It's been done.

She looked up. The opposing groups of men and women had moved closer to each other. A few brave ones were throwing out such tidbits of information as: "Oh, so you use Burbo. Do you like it? I'm having a real problem with running colors." One young man with crew cut and U.S. Drinking Team sweatshirt had delightedly surrendered his sordid pile to a cooing blonde. "Oh here. You can't put this with that, silly! One needs hot, the other cold. You men are so helpless. What would you do without us women?"

Masturbate more, thought Jenny.

He, wriggling with gratitude, helped her lift her basket of wispy lingerie from the floor to the sorting table. "Oh, you're so strong!" she cried. "You must help me move my bed. It's so close to the wall that I can hardly make it up in the morning—and I'm so fussy about unmade beds. Do you think you could? It's awfully heavy. Kingsize. With a posturepedic mattress."

He assured her there would be nothing to it and together they sorted happily away.

This successful maneuver broke the ice for the rest of them and soon the roaring washers were barely heard over the giggling of the women, the cliched cajolery of the men. Many hopeful feints were made in Jenny's direction but she waved them away. She had a standing rule: no sex while working on a painting, it put her

10

off her stroke.

When her wash was finally done, she thankfully hauled the clothes out of the drier and stuffed them into her garbage bag. She didn't care how wrinkled they got; she just wanted to get the hell home. Fending off let-me-help-ya-honeys, she plunged out the door and into the dripping darkness.

West on Beverly, across Vermont she hurried, dodging traffic and hoping that the sonofabitch who had stolen her ten-speed bike had been hit by a car. Jenny had a fantasy that the streets were gods demanding human sacrifices, the cars their priests, happy to oblige. Blood rushed into the pavement and after a proper gestation period, up sprouted baby cars. She feared cars were taking over the world. Humanity's days were numbered. But she would take a few with her when she went. There she'd be with a crowbar—denting, mashing, ripping until she was finally squashed flat by a steel-belted radial.

Engrossed in her fantasy, her luck almost ran out crossing Normandie. Jenny had been crossing with the light (not being suicidal) but neglected to look up and down the intersection. The driver, power-mad with the newly acquired privilege of turning right on red, just missed her.

"Bitch!" he yelled as his car stalled. "Why doncha watch whereya goin'?"

Still cursing and muttering, he got his car started again—then ran backwards over the curb and slammed into a purple building bearing the legend "Funky Frocks." Plate glass flew, and Jenny ducked to avoid the falling splinters.

"Fuck!" she heard the driver scream. "Fuck! God-damn slippery streets!" He stuck his beefy head out of the window and looked at her accusingly. "I thought it never rained in Los Angeles."

11

Giving her the finger, he sped off down the street.

At that point a towering figure draped in a chartreuse caftan and flapping beads came screeching from the store. "*You!*" An accusing finger pointed at Jenny. "Vandal! I'll have you in jail for this!" She grabbed Jenny with long red talons. "Henna-headed bitch!"

Stunned by the sudden assault, Jenny tried to explain, but the woman's slashing fingernails forced her to thrust the laundry bag between them, muffling her pleas. The red fingernails ripped a large hole in the bag and clothes spilled onto the street. Jenny grabbed at them, trying to stuff them into the shredded bag. As she bent over, the woman's nails tore at her. Deciding that cowardice had its merits, Jenny ran off down the street, clutching desperately at the few articles she had managed to salvage. "Whore! Communist!"

Gasping and dripping, she reached her studio. There, silhouetted beneath the streetlight, was a familiar figure. His coat was thrown open, his penis out and standing at attention.

"Shit," muttered Jenny and started into her studio. Then she thought better of it and turned around, bending over to get a better look. Looking back up at the man, she grinned and said, "You don't have to be Jewish to love Levy's."

He fled.

"Can't you sell something? Hock something?" asked Lou, as she reclined plumply on her velvet sofa.

Jenny looked at her friend with new appreciation. Such nice subcutaneous fat. Lou could live for months off it if things ever got bad—not that things would get bad for Lou Comfort. Her thing with Stirling Silver,

Famous Hollywood Producer, had already lasted for three years and showed no signs of unthinging.

Jenny sighed. "I don't have anything left to hock."

"Stereo?"

"Gone. I sold it three months ago with all my Rolling Stone albums."

"How about your bike?"

"Stolen."

"Jewelry?"

At this, Jenny had to laugh. "You must have me confused with someone else."

Lou's diamonds flashed as she lit another cigarette. "Well, I'm afraid I'm a little tight, right now. I won't get my check from Silver for another week. You know how it is." She waved a hand airily.

Jenny looked over to the corner where a shining, new twenty-five inch tv reposed. "I see," she said.

Lou blushed. "You know how it is."

"I think you already said that."

Lou sighed. "Oh, Jenny. You can be so hard on people. You know tv is one of the few things I feel up to these days.

"Yeah. I know. Your periods are so painful you can hardly move and then afterwards you're too exhausted to do anything but lie in bed. Then, just when you're starting to feel a little better you start ovulating and that lays you low again. By the time that's over you're strung out on pre-menstrual tension."

Lou sighed again. "I know. Being a woman is hard on me."

"It's hard on us all," said Jenny grimly.

"I guess I'm just more feminine than most," Lou shrugged. "A lot more so than some people I could mention." She gave Jenny a meaningful look.

Jenny groaned.

"You're crazy, you know," Lou continued. "Living

13

like you do when you've got looks like that. Why, if I had your looks there would be no end to my powers." Lou fell silent for a moment, picturing liasons with presidents, ministers of foreign powers, gas station owners. "As it is, I don't do badly at all."

Jenny looked around. That much was true. Lou certainly did not do badly. Her apartment was not quite to Jenny's taste, but it was definitely opulent. Gold leaf and crystal abounded; antiques lined the velvet-flocked walls. Lou had gum ball machines, pin ball machines, vibrating waterbeds, and mirrored ceilings. The apartment looked like a set for one of Silver's avant-garde movies, the only jarring note among that eclectic splendor being Lou herself. Instead of the sleek, chic mistress one would expect—there was Lou. Plump . . . no, call a spade a spade. Lou was fat. She wobbled when she walked and spread when she sat and her best friends could only guess at how she had managed to snare Silver. To hide her elephantine figure she was always clad in flowing caftans and dashikis. Today she was wearing silver lame and her brunette hair was piled up on her head in an intricate, sculptured mass of curls. She was barefoot (the sensuous mistress) and wore an emerald ring for emphasis on her plump, manicured toe. Resplendent was the word for Lou.

Jenny motioned to the television. "How's it going?" she asked.

Lou showed her first real sign of animation. "Oh. On 'Storm In My Heart' Kevin just found out that he has multiple sclerosis but he hasn't told Dana yet. You remember Dana's mother, Lois? She's out of the asylum now and just got a face-lift to cheer her up after the abortion but she's being blackmailed by Arthur who is thinking about running off with Barbara."

Jenny listened to the plot summaries of four other soaps in stupefied silence. When Lou finally wound up

14

breathlessly, Jenny commented, "I guess I miss a lot."

"Yes," said Lou sternly. "You should take more of an interest in the world."

Jenny decided to let that slide and just nodded, shelving her comments about the marijuana of the middle class for the next visit.

Appeased, Lou said, "Oh, by the way. I meant to tell you earlier. I saw Ken in Thrifty's yesterday."

Jenny tried to look nonchalant. "What was he doing?"

"Buying toilet paper." Noting Jenny's expression with satisfaction, she added, "He just got back from Washington. He asked about you. Wanted to know how you were. If you were married or what."

Silence.

"The man still loves you, Jenny." Lou raised her voice in irritation. "Doesn't that mean anything to you?"

Jenny's only answer was a sneer.

Scowling, Lou continued, "Jenny, you're the most cold-hearted woman I've ever known. It isn't natural. But I know you're not frigid because you're always sleeping around with God-knows-what-all."

"Only men." Jenny corrected. "And only in between paintings."

"So you say," Lou retorted. "Sick, that's what it is. All that loveless sex. Just what have you got against love, anyway?"

"Love. Hah." Jenny snorted. "Just another word for mind-rape."

"Some people think otherwise," Lou said.

"Yeah, I know. Love makes the world go round and all that shit." Jenny ranted on, "Love. Ha. Love's been the excuse for more crimes than religion and I'll bet it's caused almost as much misery. The Great Rationale! It gives you the right to inflict any wound, any humiliation you want to on someone. Fuck love! I'll take good old honest hate and loathing any day!"

She fumed to a stop, then added, "And don't talk to me about Ken!" Almost as an afterthought, she remembered the main reason for her visit. "Say, Lou. Can I use your bathtub?"

Later, clean and calm, Jenny sat at the kitchen table with Lou trying to figure out where all her money had gone. Not that there had been all that much to start with. Lou's excellence with figures (the numerical kind) had been of help to Jenny on many an occasion for Jenny couldn't add two and two and come up with the right answer. In school she had flunked math twice before she finally passed it. "There's not a college in the country that'll take her," the principal told her hand-wringing mother. "You're lucky she's gifted."

It wasn't Jenny's fault; she had tried everything. Memorization, reason, logic. Today, at thirty, she still didn't know her multiplication tables.

"Are you sure there was no other income?" Lou asked, chewing worriedly at the end of her pencil.

"I'm sure," Jenny moaned.

Lou shook her head. "Well, as I see it, your average monthly income this year has been one hundred eighty-six dollars and forty-two cents. Are you sure you're not holding anything back? I don't see how you can exist on that."

Jenny looked at the row of figures representing a summer of doing pastel portraits of tourists at the Farmer's Market, some illustrations for a Wilshire Boulevard ad agency, the proceeds from the sale of three paintings. "That's it."

"God," Lou said, "I'm glad I have no talent. I don't think I could take it. It depresses me just hearing all these sad stories. No," Lou said, still shaking her head. "It's what I was afraid of. You're not solvent."

That night Jenny had a dream about Ken. He was standing at the church altar, wearing a crash helmet and a pink organdy apron, singing "We Shall Overcome." Sushi was there. He was the best man. Lou was the maid of honor. The minister was Pablo Picasso.

"Before I begin this ceremony," Picasso said, "I must make sure that you understand the gravity of the situation." He looked piercingly at Jenny. "Never paint from dark to light, always vice versa. Ready?"

"Ready as I'll ever be," Jenny said.

Ken handed her a burned tuna noodle casserole instead of a ring and said, "You'll sure as hell have to do better than this.

Picasso leaned over, looked at it and said, "I agree. It definitely needs more green."

At that, her mother jumped up crying, "Oh, my baby! My little baby girl!"

Then her father said, "Don't cry, Momma. You're not losing a daughter—you're gaining a signed, numbered lithograph."

The choir started to sing "Oh, Baby, Don't You Loose Your Lip On Me," and Jenny woke up.

She got up the next morning with a familiar sense of panic. Nothing was resolved—she was still poor, and, as was her usual routine in moments of desperation, she began to worry about losing her creativity. It was probably disappearing. Fast. It happened, Jenny knew. She remembered histories of artists who had shone brilliantly during their youth and then burned out in their forties like meteors falling through the atmosphere. Sometimes she didn't really care if she died young—which was always a possibility considering the way she lived. But, please God, don't let her creativity precede her.

Back in Detroit in art school, one of her teachers had called her his "Little Rembrandt," and after his fashion had reviled her with his foulest curses, his most violent tirades. "Mediocrity should be ignored," he had growled, "but excellence should be given the utmost attention." There was no doubt that his psychology was right on target. Sometimes she had sat sobbing at her easel as he screamed, but always she continued to work.

Oh, he had fired her, that man, and by senior year she was painting every night until two or three in the morning, getting up at six to carry her brushes to class where she would begin again. "Supergirl," some students called her. "Super-Artist," she had snarled back.

The end result of such a masochistic schedule should have come as no surprise to her—but it did. As she lay in the hospital with tubes protruding from every orifice, she had rasped to the intern, "What?" and, "Why?"

"Oh, it's a simple diagnosis," he had told her proudly, cheerfully. "Pneumonia. Exhaustion." Patting her sheeted leg, he added, "Better take it easy, girl. By the way, you doing anything special tonight?"

Never again, she had sworn to herself, fending off advances by interns, residents, and orderlies. She had learned something—that she could be driven farther than she could safely go. It wouldn't happen again. She remembered the horror stories of an alcoholic Modigliani, a leprous Gauguin, a mad Van Gogh and swore that it wasn't going to happen to her. If fame and fortune were to come her way, Jenny decided, she would be there to meet it—fat, sober, and healthy.

She told her teacher to find another little Rembrandt, this one was moving to California.

"Only six months until your degree!" her mother screamed. "Six months! And after I told all of the relatives, all my friends that you were going to be an art teacher! A mother has got a right to expect a return on her investment. And what have I got now? An undegreed nothing!" She was still for a moment, then said, "Oh well. Thank God you're pretty. Someone will marry you."

Jenny's father was slumped dejectly in his chair. He had heard it all before. He and Jenny rarely spoke unless it was either snowing or raining and then one would say, "Look. It's raining." And the other would say, "How about that!"

Jenny's mother wasn't finished. "Tell me," she commanded. "Are you still a virgin?"

"Mom, I haven't been a virgin in four years," said Jenny with a big smile.

Her mother looked at her, aghast, seeing Jenny's stock plummet. She caught her breath and howled, "Oh God! Not even decent. Did you hear that, Roy? Your daughter's been doing it!"

The pale, gray man smiled vaguely. "Oh, don't begrudge the kid a little fun, Marge."

Jenny walked over to him and gave him a hug. "Bye, Dad. I'll send you a post card from Disney-land."

Glum thoughts. Glum thoughts. Try to look on the bright side, Jenny told herself. *Danse Macabre*

was almost finished. Tonight, maybe, with a little bit of hard work. It had been almost three weeks of painting all day and usually far into the night and she was getting sick of it. The painting itself had become a tyrant.

Once she read the words of an art critic. That non-painting expert had explained the creative urge to one and all. "The artist must create out of a vacuum—he must pull reality out of nothingness in order to fill his own emotional void. He creates merely to hide his own fear of nonexistence."

Bullshit, Jenny thought. Her painting was spontaneous—uncontrollable, like a sneeze. It was something she didn't plan until she found herself in front of her easel, brush in hand. The critics irritated her with their posturing, intellectualized attempts to explain away creativity. They reminded her of all those other men (and they were always men) writing books on female sexuality and female orgasm. The grasshopper describing life as a gnat.

She started painting.

Sushi dropped by around noon. "Hear honorable redhead in bad way," he singsonged as he bowed himself through the door. SuperJap carrying an ice chest.

"What's that?" Jenny asked, putting down her brush with a welcoming smile.

"Smoked fish. From honorable parents' fish market in Japanese ghetto." He groaned as he set it down. "Brain food. Also . . ." He opened the chest and lifted out a bottle. "Scotch. Sushi and redhead get honorable buzz on."

Jenny lept for the bottle.

Jenny had met Sushi years back in a disreputable

bar on Eighth Street known for its vice squad arrests and superb graffiti. "Wanna screw?" he had leered right after introducing himself. She had looked at him in shock (she was new to Los Angeles at the time), taking in his wispy beard and rat's nest hair: the very picture of Oriental lechery.

"Uh—no, thank you," she replied as she looked desperately for the bouncer.·

"What a relief!" he said. "I'm impotent anyway."

It broke her up.

They got gloriously drunk together and he took her home at closing time and fed her raw mushrooms and saki—but oddly enough, they never slept together. Perhaps they both felt that their friendship was too important to risk. The instant they discovered that both were artists they fell on each other like long lost friends and talked painting until dawn. He showed her his works—soft, gentle canvasses in pastel colors. "Very feminine," she cracked. "Very Oriental," he corrected. Jenny recognized that Sushi had what artists desire most in their own talent—technical ability.

Their friendship had continued through the years, surviving each other's changes in finances, politics, and bed partners. Jenny eventually discovered, upon many a good female authority, that Sushi was far from impotent.

So Jenny learned another lesson. Beware the man who boasts of his virility. Most of it is in his mouth.

"Still raining, eh?" Jenny said, tippling on her Scotch.

"Raining? What makes you think that?" Sushi was a native Californian. He ignored any weather conditions that did not meet the criteria of the

L.A. Chamber of Commerce.

"You're dripping on my mattress," Jenny observed.

"Just a slight mist."

Sushi, it developed, was in a depressed state. Angela Hearthside, the flower child he had been living with, was in an advanced state of pregnancy and it was getting on his nerves. "Nag, nag, nag. All day long. She's driving me crazy. She won't clean, won't cook, won't fillet Momma's flounder—I just can't stand it any more."

But Jenny sympathized with Angela. "You probably wouldn't be any too chipper, either, if you had to sleep on your back all the time. Serves you right for getting her pregnant."

Sushi looked hurt. "Birth control is the woman's job. She's the one who gets pregnant."

"But I notice that it's the man who screams when he's inconvenienced," Jenny observed.

There was a brief silence while recriminations hung heavily in the air. Then Sushi sighed and motioned towards *Danse Macabre.* "It's going well, I see."

"Yeah. It's coming along."

Sushi shuffled his sandaled feet uncomfortably. "This exhibit will be the turning point for you. I'm certain of it."

Jenny snorted.

"Really, Jen." Democratically, he added, "You're better than me, you know."

"I know."

"I just can't see why you're having such a hard time of it." Sushi was shaking his head in bewilderment.

"You can't, huh?"

"No. I can't. You're so obviously good. Maybe

you'll even be considered great some day. You
could be the first great woman artist."

Jenny went white. "First great woman artist, my
ass! You act like there haven't been any great women
painters! There have been, plenty of them, but you male
bastards refuse to admit it. Remember that flap at the
Metropolitan Museum about that so-called David—
the portrait of Charlotte du Val d'Ognes? It was supposed to be one of David's greatest works. Shit. The
critics had regular orgasms over it. Then all of a sudden surprise, surprise! It turned out to have been painted by a woman! Ah, the shame and chagrin in the
art world. Suddenly everybody started talking about
"weaknesses," "flaws," "inferior workmanship."
That about a painting that had been a masterpiece
one week earlier. And that wasn't the only case.
There have been so many others. Paintings attributed to Franz Hals, Tintoretto, Rembrandt—all considered masterpieces until it was discovered that wom-
en did them. So don't hand me that crap about me
being the first great woman artist. There have been
plenty others and you know it. There always were.
They all had to paint under assumed names."

Sushi sat blinking at this onslaught. "Good grief,
Jen. Don't get so uptight. It's not my fault."

Jenny slowed from a boil to a simmer. "Oh hell,
Sushi. I'm sorry I yelled at you like that. It's just that
I'm so tired of the whole damn thing."

In more optimistic days Jenny had decided to start
at the top in trying to secure an exhibit for her works.
There were two galleries, both located in Beverly Hills,
which qualified: Alfred R. Howell's and Harold Dodd's.
Jenny had tried Howell's first; he had frequently shown
himself to be sympathetic to new talent. "My God!"
he had exclaimed as he looked at her slides. "Real live

painting! I haven't seen paint put on canvas in over two years!"

Jenny knew.

Howell's current show was called *Garbage Can Art from the Inner City*, and before that he had exhibited painted, live hermaphrodites. Before that, the infamous show of chicken droppings on colored chiffon. *Time* magazine had swooped down and done a cover story on him (Howell Rampant, surrounded by chickens). Sugar Daddy of the Art World, they had called him.

Sugar Daddy had promised her an exhibit in June, but then he had called her two weeks before it was to open with apologies. "You see, dear. There are these two delicious boys from New York who cover themselves with gold paint and sing Guy Lombardo hits. Besides," he had added, "painting is passe."

Then Dodd's. That great man would not lower himself to even look at her slides. "I don't exhibit ladies' art, honey. Too decorative. Pastel. Art is hard-edge this year." Then he had pinched her and asked her for a date.

Pride smarting (along with the pinched rump) she had called Sushi to cry on his shoulder. "Poor baby." he had commiserated. "Poor, mistreated thing."

And then, just as fast as his little bow legs could carry him, he sped to Dodd's, slides in hand.

His exhibit opened one month later.

The gallery brochure (written by Dodd himself) had cooed over Sushi's "delicate adherence to the decorative tradition of Oriental Art. Soft. Glowing. Muted. colors. Not for Sushi Takamoto the harsh combinations of the New York school! His paintings do not turn away from beauty—but then, Sushi Takamoto is an Artist!"

A choice, not an echo, Jenny had snorted when she read it.

24

Sushi's ascent to fame was as expected. Dodd's was the equivalent of the Good Housekeeping Seal of Approval. Soon Sushi was on every wall—every wealthy wall.

"You ought to get out more, Jenny," he was saying. "Get some air. Some sun."

"Air? Sun? Looked outside lately? Shit! The smog knocks you down and then you drown in the street. Not to mention the fact that they've declared war on me out there."

"They? They? Who's they?"

"Oh, the same they, I guess, that keep the street lights burning. The ones that remove the dead dogs from the gutter. The theys that are supposed to rescue damsels in distress."

"Oh. Those theys."

"Yeah. So don't talk to me about going outside. Freaky things happen to me every time I step out the door."

"Sounds paranoid to me." Sushi looked suspiciously at her from underneath raised eyebrows.

"Yeah, well you know what *they* say about paranoids. Sometimes they really do have enemies."

"Jenny, Jenny. It sounds like you're losing your nerve. And I've always admired you for being so courageous, brave, and all that. Don't disappoint me."

Jenny looked at him with a faint smile. "It wouldn't be the first time I've disappointed someone."

Just about the only person she had never disappointed was her father. He expected nothing.

"Say, Sushi," Jenny said hopefully. "Hard times, right? You couldn't see your way into loaning me, say, a hundred dollars? Enough for me to make it until my exhibit."

He looked stunned, then stammered, "Uh—well—uh everything's sort of tied up right now, you know? And

25

my stock hasn't been looking too good lately—you
know the way things have been going on the Street . . ."
he trailed off.

"Yeah, well. I get the message."

Sushi waved his hand weakly. "You know how it is."

Jenny said, "I'm learning fast."

By five o'clock the next day she had finished *Danse
Macabre*.

"Oh, bitchin'!" she laughed as she slapped on the
final strokes. "Super fan-fucking-tastic!" And it was.
Danse Macabre was excellent. What Jenny had tried
to do had come very near to succeeding—and in the
end, that was the most an artist could ever hope for.

Was the face on the middle corpse out of proportion? Everything had been distorted, true, but perhaps that particular face was out of proportion in
the wrong way. And the backgrounds. Too drab? Too
neutralized? But if it had been just a little more in-
tense it would have overpowered the dancing figures
in the foreground.

Jenny had taken the painting as far as it could go.
She knew that the most difficult part of painting was
knowing when to stop. Any corrections—a change of
feeling or of vision—would have to be done on the next
canvas. And when it came right down to it, that was one
of the rewards of painting—that you may have failed
but you always got another chance.

She turned her back on the canvas and addressed herself to her present problems in life.

She was hungry. She was horny. It was a bad—but
not unfamiliar—situation. There was some more of
Sushi's smoked fish left but she had eaten so much

26

of it already that she expected to break out in scales any minute. A search through her pockets came up with only thirty cents—not enough to buy salt for sardines.

They say a drowning man's life passes before his eyes. It was also true in the case of starving women. A motley mob paraded by: Billy, Hank, Nancy Mae, Ken, her mother. They all lurched by hissing and cackling, "Ha. We told you. You'd get yours, we said, and we were right, kid, you did. Think you're so smart. Well, we told you . We warned you. This is what you get, asshole, for fighting city hall."

Jenny was five years old again, standing under her mother's grape arbor with Billy. "Show me yours and I'll show you mine," he said. She did, pulling down her blue jeans and underpants, exposing twin pink petals. Billy goggled.

"Okay. Now it's your turn," she said.

Billy just kept staring out of his six-year-old eyes.

"Come on, Billy. Now I get to see your thing."

Billy took one final look and then ran off down the alley leaving her (not for the last time) with her pants down.

Then she was seven. She got Larry (age seven) in his parents' refurbished basement. He showed her everything he had—but the thrill was gone.

She was ten, standing by the kitchen sink, a pink apron around her waist. Her mother's hands were immersed in oily gray water. Flecks of bloated food floated past dismal soap suds. Her mother interrupted a hummed version of "I Could Have Danced All Night" to say to Jenny, "Always wash the pots and pans last. That keeps your dishwater clean. When I first got married I did them first—then halfway through the dishes I had to drain the water out and start all over. I've learned a lot since then."

The water ran down the drain with a sucking sound,

27

leaving the trap filled with the soggy, sordid remnants of the meal.

She was thirteen. She had just woke up to find her pajamas and sheets bloody. "I'm dying," she thought.

Her mother found her scrubbing her pajamas in the bathroom sink, crying and shaking.

"What's that?" Her mother grabbed the streaked pajamas out of the pink water. "Oh my baby! My little baby! A woman now. All grown up!" She gave Jenny one of her own Kotex and told her how wonderful it all was.

At dinner her mother announced to her father, "Well, Roy. Our little girl's not a little girl any more." Her face was heavy with secrecy and importance.

Jenny's father just looked sad.

She was fifteen. A word from the grapevine suggested that Nancy Mae—yes, frizzy-haired, bow-legged, flat-chested Nancy Mae—was pregnant. With child. A bun in the oven. A real live baby was growing in there. Now that was grown up! But Nancy Mae refused to go into details. "Come on, Nancy Mae," they all begged. "Where? Who was it?" Was it in the back seat of a car? In Nancy Mae's basement playroom? At Bernie's party? They couldn't bring themselves to ask what they really wanted to know. Did it feel good? How long did it take? Did she come?

Nancy Mae finally went off to visit an "aunt" in Phoenix, Arizona, and returned six months later, flat and mute. On graduation day, Jenny leaned over and whispered in her ear, "Where? Who?" But Nancy Mae just smiled and collected her diploma.

Jenny was sixteen and trying to fall in love. She wanted to be just like everybody else but it wasn't working.

Hank Raunche, the only slightly-pimply captain of the football team, asked her to go see "Breakfast at

Tiffany's" with him at the Blue Sky Drive-In. She quiv-
ered. He was the Fair Maid's Dream, God's Gift to Vag-
inas—cutting a swath through the sophomore class,
leaving a trail of broken hearts and busted hymens in
his wake. Her big chance.

All through the picture, while Audrey Hepburn got
in and out of taxicabs, his tongue ran in and out of her
ear. He clawed at her breasts, raked at her thighs, but
Jenny just wondered how in the world Audrey managed
to get all those taxis. Breathing heavily, he rasped, "Oh,
Jenny baby, you're the one for me."

She offered him her Hershey bar, and said, "Ever
thought of joining the Marines, Hank?"

She was eighteen and finally losing her virginity in
the back of Ken's father's Lincoln Continental. It hurt.
After it was over the only emotion she felt was anger
that she had been led to expect so much. All men were
liars. She looked dismally at the wet spot on the seat.
"What are you going to tell your dad that is?" she
asked.

Ken was busily tucking himself in. "Buttered popcorn," he said. "I'll tell him that you dropped your
buttered popcorn."

What to do? What to do? This was Thursday, Silver's
night to howl at Lou's. No hope there. An idea that
had been tumble-drying in her mind had finally emerged
wrinkle-free (as they say on Wilshire Boulevard). She
could panhandle in MacArthur Park. Why not? Everybody else did. It was just another rung of the ladder of
success that she was destined to descend before she
bottomed out.

She checked out the door for muggers and saw that
the coast was clear. Leaving the studio she noticed glumly that the hole in her umbrella was getting bigger.

The rain was still at it (Los Angeles was nothing if
not persistent) and after a sad look at her U.S. Keds,

she started walking. She managed to get without incident to Vermont but there it happened. A frail-looking old woman darted out from under an awning, pinched her painfully on the arm, and said, "The scarlet woman of Babylon knoweth no redemption." She then grabbed Jenny's umbrella and skipped nimbly down the street.

Jenny stared morosely after her. Shit, she muttered. Life was going by right on schedule. The war was still on. The rest of her journey to MacArthur Park was plagued by skidding cars and urinating poodles.

MacArthur Park lay at the intersection of Alvarado and Wilshire, a bright spot of green amid the city's gray concrete. Tall eucalyptus trees which usually grew out of earth parched by desert conditions were dripping and molding in the soaked green grass. Palm trees stood in aloof clusters giving neither shade nor comfort to man or beast.

As Jenny entered the park she looked hopefully in the small lake for ducks but none were to be seen. They were all hiding under the docks at the boat rental or had been taken home by hungry senior citizens for a menu change from their staple of dog food. A few of these senior citizens still hopefully prowled the lake's perimeter, club in hand.

The cars whizzed by on Wilshire, headed for the financial district, and as a particularly large limousine would pass, the oldies would give a Bronx cheer. "BBBZZZZATTTT!" for a Lincoln. "BBRRRWW-WWIER!" for a Rolls. "BBLLLFFFT!" to a Bentley. They stood, bent by arthritis, waving and shaking their clubs at the water's edges, but unbowed.

Looking at them, Jenny didn't feel quite so alone. Artists weren't the only ones despised by society; children and old people ran a close second.

Positioning herself under a shuddering eucalyptus she held out her palm and tried to look pitiful. "Spare change?" she said hopefully. "Anybody got spare change?"

"Hey, scab!" came a gravelly voice behind her. "Vamoose! Move-hay your ass-hay!"

Jenny turned to see three people of indeterminate sex and assorted colors, all wearing naturals. "This is our spot," the largest of the he/she/its said.

"Just what do you mean, your spot?"

"Just what I said, bitch. Our spot." The voice lowered threateningly. "Bug off or I'll report you to the local."

Jenny was puzzled. "Local what?"

The three looked at each other meaningfully. "Do you think . . . " began the short one. "I'll bet," answered the medium one. The tall he/she/it produced a card. "Bartholomew H. Harris. Panhandler's Local No. 417."

"Oh, shit," Jenny said.

"Look, Babe." It was now identified as a male. "The by-laws clearly state that any scab found panhandling without sanction and protection of the union is to be chased ass forth with."

"Aw. Can't you bend the rules a little?"

The short one scowled. "If we bend them for one, next thing you know, we'll be bending them for all. And then you know what we'd have?"

"No."

"Anarchy," the three hissed together.

Jenny decided to give it one last try. "But you see I honestly didn't know anything about a union. Really."

Bartholomew H. Harris growled, "Ignorance of the law is no excuse."

Jenny admitted defeat and beat a strategic retreat. She took shelter underneath a barbershop awning, howling, "Aw, FFUUUUUUCCKK!"

"That's not a nice thing for a lady to say," said a man's voice from behind her.

She turned around. He had just come out of the

barbershop, trimmed and tweedy. He wore a tweed
suit, a tweed hat, and if tweed umbrellas had been
manufactured, he would have carried one. She half
expected to see sheep gamboling on his trousers.

"So what's it to ya?" she snarled. Jenny wasn't
always creative.

He started to reply, then looked at her more carefully. Her wet clothes were clinging to her body. "Ah,
nice day, isn't it?" he said perkily. "Sun's going to come
out any minute now. Come here often?"

"Humph," answered Jenny.

"Let me introduce myself. My name is Brian Hampshire-Landrace. I'm thirty one, I teach at UCLA. I'm a
Pisces. Very sensitive. I doubt seriously if there is an oil
shortage. Are you a secretary? A stewardess? What sign
are you? Who do you like best—Rod McKuen or Neil
Diamond? Did you see 'The Exorcist?' I have munici-
pal bonds and a partial bridge on my lower left quad-
rant. I believe in letting it all hang out."

He paused long enough for Jenny to come out of
her coma and snap, "Just what the hell do you teach?
Current American Trivia?"

The rain was slowing and Jenny decided that it was
time to move on. "Good bye," she said. "Don't forget
to get it on, too."

"Wait. Don't go," he cried desperately, chasing
after her. "I was going to ask you to lunch!"

The Mexican restaurant was typical. It was staffed
by French and German waiters with a headwaiter from
Spain—the only Mexicans were the busboys and dish-
washers. The walls were covered in hot pink and lime
green burlap (a combination which the Sunday magazine section had declared was "south of the border"
that year) and papier mache donkeys hung drunkenly
from the ceiling. Paintings of bullfighters and blue-eyed

Mexican senoritas abounded.

However, as did most artists, Jenny had a strong stomach.

She sat back contentedly against the carved wooden chair and listened to Brian Hampshire-Landrace tell her all about the culturally disadvantaged—which, it developed, he taught. "A case of the self-fulfilling prophecy," he was saying.

"Ummm," Jenny answered, biting into a beef enchilada dripping with cheese, green onions, and ripe olives.

"You know what that is—the self-fulfilling prophecy? A real sociological truism if ever there was one. You know, if you constantly tell a race—say, the Blacks— that they are only capable of a certain limited level of achievement, then after a time that race starts believing it themselves. People tend to become what their environment expects them to become. Their view of themselves is fashioned by what other people think about them. For years the Blacks believed that they weren't capable of higher thought—that they were great athletes, passionate, animalistic, and dumb. After all, wasn't that what the white folks said and they should know? So we got all those Sonny Listons but no Ph.D's. But now, with Black Power, the Black is becoming more aware, and the number of educated, producing, creating Black men is skyrocketing. About time, too."

"Ummm. Prejudice is an awful thing," Jenny said as she buttered another tortilla.

He smiled at her. "But I shouldn't worry your pretty little head with stuff like that. Good food, isn't it?"

"Best I've had in ages." Jenny burped slightly and smiled with pleasure.

"I like to see a woman who enjoys eating. It means she's natural. Close to her life forces."

"Right. Can I have another marguerita?"

After ordering it (her fourth) he continued, "A

33

woman, that is, a *real* woman, is like a river. She
flows gently, in harmony with the truths of creation.
She doesn't have to do because she is. She is Man's
mediator with God. She is the quiet pool of strength
from which he returns refreshed."

Jenny eyed him suspiciously for a moment, then
went back to her enchilada.

Brian droned on. "I'm all for this Woman's Lib, now,
don't get me wrong. I'm liberal. Voted for McGovern.
Equal pay for equal work, I say. Damn right! (Please excuse my French. I usually try not to swear in front of
ladies.) But the plain, unbiased truth of the matter is
that women just aren't suited for certain kinds of work.
Jobs that require important decisions, for instance. Their
minds are different. It's because of their hormones."

"Hormones?" Jenny looked up. "Oh, yes. Hormones.
Say, could I have some dessert? An eclair?"

It promptly arrived.

"And," Brian continued, "there are certain times
when, uh, a woman just isn't up to things. When she's
not feeling too well. I certainly wouldn't want a woman's hand on the red phone in the White House at a
time like that."

"You're so right," Jenny muttered, lapping up choc-
olate with her tongue. "So right. Besides. Who would
take care of the children?"

"Exactly!" He banged his fist on the table. "I'm so
glad we see eye to eye."

"Oh, we do. We do." Jenny smiled. "Do you think
you could order me another eclair?"

The rain had stopped when he drove her home. She
took it as an omen. She was always taking things as
omens when she wanted a good excuse for doing something she had planned on doing anyway. "Come on in,"
she purred as she held the door open. Into my parlor,

heh heh.

He looked around in shock. "This is where you live?"

"You could call it that."

He stared at the canvasses stacked against the wall. "Did you do those?"

"Yes."

"Well. I see you like to paint."

"Yes. I like to paint."

"Well, I'll admit that I don't know anything about art but I know what I like."

Jenny smiled. "Somehow I knew you were going to say that."

"Maybe you have talent. Why don't you take a night course over at the city college and see if you can develop it?"

"That's a great idea."

He looked at her approvingly. "I admire creative women. My mother does terrific things with those mosaic kits you get at Newberry's." He peered closely at *Danse Macabre.* "You need to study anatomy, I would say. Look at that man's body there. It's all out of proportion."

"It's supposed to be," Jenny said. "He's been disemboweled."

Brian went white. "Good God! A woman shouldn't be thinking about things like that!"

Finally. An opening. She slipped off her turtleneck. "Then why don't you help me think about something else?"

He was shocked initially, but quick on the uptake. He tore at his clothes, paring rapidly down to his magenta shorts and matching socks. "Well, Jenny. You're really an unusual girl."

"Yes," she answered. She was already naked and stretched out invitingly on the mattress.

Argyle flew. "Must be this bohemian life you

lead. Remind me sometime to tell you about the
Trobriand Islanders."

"Right." Her smile grew broader as she noticed his
erection. Thank God. Nothing annoyed her more than
wasted time. He slipped off his shorts and presented
himself proudly to her.

"Nice," she commented. "Very nice. Come here,
lover."

As a lover, Brian Hampshire-Landrace wasn't bad.
Predictable, maybe, but not bad. On a scale of one to
five Jenny gave him a four. He had read all the right
books, perfected his technique, and learned a little
self-control, but he lacked abandon. He spent the advised amount of time on her left breast, copied that
with the right, then moved on down to her soft, round
belly. After a brief sojourn there he went for broke.

He entered carefully, his fingers first asking per-
mission. Jenny liked polite men. At the pumping itself he was slow and steady—Aesop's turtle. Jenny
closed her eyes and enjoyed, enjoyed.

Later, as he had a post-coital smoke (with a pipe,
natch) he shook his head worriedly. "Do you ever get
the feeling that you're losing control of things?"

"What are you talking about?" She rubbed her foot
against his.

"Oh, never mind. I guess it wasn't important."

She leaned over and patted his penis affectionately.
It had shrunk back, almost invisible, into its furry nest.
In its relaxed state it was quite small and he had asked
her anxiously if it was big enough. She was amused. It
had been her experience that in bed (as in the Kingdom
of God) the least became the greatest.

He nibbled at her left breast. "I'd like you to meet
my mother."

"I'd really rather not."

"Oh." He moved to her right breast. "You'd like her. She's very arty. She'll show you how to make mosaic coffee tables and molded salads."

"No."

"You can't go on being a loner all your life, you know."

"So what's wrong with being a loner?"

"It's against nature. God's plan."

"What isn't these days?"

"Seriously. Stop that. I can't concentrate while you do that. Don't you feel that it's about time you settled down?"

"I am settled down. I've lived here for four years."

"That's not what I meant."

Jenny rolled over in disgust. "Aw, shit. This happens every time. I can't get a fuck any more without having to listen to a lecture, too."

"Do you have to talk like that?" He looked hurt.

"Yes. It relieves my pent-up frustrations. Isn't it about time you went home? The streetlights are on."

He jumped up and dressed in a huff. "Well. Try to be nice to someone and this is what you get. I was interested in you. I could maybe even love you. And then you treat me like this. I won't stand for it. What do you think I am, anyway?"

He slammed the door behind him. A few green and brown pieces of tweedy lint hung suspended in the air for a moment, then drifted slowly to the floor.

Sleep came that night in scattered dreams. The worst: Brian sat atop a flagpole on the UCLA campus. Beneath, Jenny wore an apron and puttered around marigolds.

"A woman's place is in the home," Brian called down

to her.

"Yes, dear," she called back. "What kind of home would you prefer?"

"A home for the mentally infirm," he answered.

"Yes, dear," she yelled.

"It's almost sunrise. Send up the flag."

"Yes, dear." Jenny shook a flag out of her apron pocket, attached it to the pulley rope, and sent it up. Brian grabbed it, held it out so the wind could catch it, and sang "God Bless America."

The flag whipped in the breeze, spread out, and revealed itself to be a long green snake stretched across a field of red and white stripes. Beneath the snake were the words, "Don't tread on me."

She finally awoke starving. Her stomach had gotten its first taste of real food in ages and now it wanted more.

It was now Friday and the chances were good that Silver had left Lou's apartment for he rarely stayed the night. Envisioning eggs frying in butter and coffee laden with cream, she decided to chance it and hopefully, briskly, walked to Lou's. But when she arrived, there Stirling Silver was lounged, luxuriant in a velvet jump suit on Lou's stuffed gold sofa, watching "Hollywood Squares."

"Well, well," he said sarcastically. "Here's Picasso. All set to mooch another meal?"

The detestation was mutual. "Hi, fart," saluted Jenny. "How's the wife and kiddies?"

"The kiddies are well, thank you. The wife is having menopause."

Jenny scowled. "You're putting on a little weight, I see."

"Only to match my expanding stock portfolio." Contented.

As in the way of all things, the rich were getting

38

richer. Silver's latest picture was the highly acclaimed *Albert—An Odyssey*. It was the account of a crisis in the life of Albert, a four-inch-long dark brown turd who lived in a three-hole outhouse owned by Jonothan Robertson, a soybean farmer. Albert was in love with Roxanne, a delicate mustard-colored creature who dwelt two holes over. In order to become worthy of Roxanne's love (there were many suitors owing to the large number of hired hands employed by Farmer Robertson) Albert embarked on an inward quest to become the most perfect turd in the world. The musical score of the picture had been written by a leading rock musician and the voice-overs were done by a gravelly poet. There were a lot of arty, unfocused shots of defecating backsides. The critics had raved, calling *Albert—An Odyssey* a metaphorical account of the soul in its quest for God." Silver (to give the devil his due) had called it a piece of shit and had new carpeting installed in his manse.

Smiling down at her from his lofty perch shared only by the critically acclaimed and richly rewarded, Silver asked, "Get any lately?"

"None of your business."

"How's the painting going?"

"Fine."

"Hear you've got an exhibit coming up. Where?"

This time she had to answer. Silver had bought paintings before and might again. "At the Pearce Gallery," she sighed.

"Never heard of it."

"Neither has the art critic at the *L.A.Journal.*" Talking about her morals, she decided, was preferable to talking about her disappointments. She was embarrassed by Pearce's lack of reputation, but she knew she would be even more embarrassed if the gallery had been better known. Pearce, kindly soul though he might be, was still exhibiting paintings of saucer-eyed children and purple sunsets.

"Heh, heh. Not exactly raking it in, are you?" Silver loved to rub it in.

Jenny flamed. "So who says affluence is any indication of artistic merit!"

"This is Hollywood, sweets."

Silver took his cigar out of his mouth, an indication that he was getting ready for a long speech. "Has it ever occurred to you, Jenny, that the way you live—hand to mouth, day by day—is in actuality the intentional fulfillment of a basically masochistic personality? Ah, now. Let me finish. Don't make noises like that. It's rude. I know what you think about Freud but he said that women are all motivated by masochism—and by the very nature of your rebellion you are proving him right. So even in your combat-booted nonconformity you are still the feminine female you so despise." He stopped triumphantly, his allegorical foot on her allegorical neck.

"Oh, balls, Silver." Jenny knew why she lived like that. She was a sensualist. She had never met an artist who wasn't. There had always been that difference between her and other people.

Her teachers issued dire warnings to her parents. A dreamer, they intoned solemnly. You're going to have trouble with this kid. She can't keep her mind on the long division, the capitals of foreign countries—the important things in life. What good is a person who doesn't know that Franklin Pierce was the fourteenth president of the United States? You'd better do something fast, they warned. Jenny wasn't adjusting.

When Jenny was ten her parents took her to a psychologist. He was a large, friendly man who put her in a small room, showed her pictures, and told her to write stories about them. Instead, she copied the pictures

40

but she rearranged the compositions so that they looked more attractive to her. Then he showed her rows of dots and asked her to place them in different orders—which she did, all results being wildly asymmetrical. When he asked her why she arranged them thus she just shrugged her shoulders and said, "I dunno. Guess they look better that way. Not so dull."

She enjoyed the ink blot test. She asked him if he had a spare set he could give her and if he didn't could she copy them.

The tests completed, he left her in the room while he went to talk to her parents. She never found out what he had said to them, but soon afterwards she was given a beginner's set of oil paint, some canvasses, and a sketch pad. And soon after that Jenny realized that her mother was beginning to hate her.

"I'm just telling you these things for your own good, Jenny," Silver explained righteously.

"Sure you are, Silver. Every time a man insults a woman, he's doing it for her own good."

"The truth is hard to accept, I know. But don't fight it. Lord knows I didn't like admitting my feelings about my mother to myself but my analyst showed me that my mind would be healthier because of it. And know what? He was right. The minute I admitted to myself that my mother was a dominating, castrating bitch I began to feel better."

"Oh, God, Silver. Please don't tell me about your mother. I've had my fill of mothers for the week." Jenny threw a hopeful glance at the kitchen. No sign of food; no sign of Lou; no rescue in sight.

He scowled. "Never interested in anybody but yourself, are you?"

"So? Who's interested in me?" Jenny was beginning to grow angry at Silver's constant jibes.

"Are you kidding? I've seen you shed men like fleas.

41

Men who loved you, wanted to marry you. Don't tell
me they weren't interested!"

"The fuck they were," Jenny said. "If my pussy
ever grew over solid you'd find out just how interested
they were!"

Silver looked prim. "You ought to clean up your
mouth. Act like a lady."

"Through with your Norman Mailer imitation?
'Cause if you are, I'd like to tell you something. You're
a goddamn bigot!"

That hit Silver where it hurt. "What? Bigot? You
bitch! I'll have you know that I've done two documen-
taries on the wretched plight of the American Indian
and I give more money every year to disadvantaged minority groups than Standard Oil pays taxes! I'm as
broadminded as they come. I'm certainly no bigot. And
anyway, what's that got to do with your out-house
mouth?"

"Just this, Chief Bleeding-Heart. You walk around
screeching about how liberal you are and then when it
comes to the rights of women you're just a closet conservative! Sure you donated to Angela Davis' defense
fund. You wanted her freed so she could go home and
cook the grits. I'm getting sick of you up-tight, pin-
assed men running my life. I can't get a decent gallery
to show my work. They're all owned by men. And
that's all they exhibit. Men! It's like the John Birch Society screaming, 'Buy American!' You all give me a
pain, Silver. You can't see beyond a woman's tits. You
bastards are so fucking eager to get back to the breast
that you've forgotten that there's a human being
attached!"

Silver gasped. "Now wait a minute. Just wait a
minute. You're one hundred per cent, totally, categori-
cally wrong. I love women for themselves. I truly do.
Look at Lou. She's no beauty and yet I love her. I treat

her like a queen."

"Yeah. But did you ever try treating her like a human being?"

"Now, Jenny. You're barking up the wrong tree. Men hold women to be among the most precious things on earth. Why, look at all the love sonnets men have written about women." He leaned back, closed his eyes, and reverently recited, "She walks in beauty like the night of cloudless climes and starry skies . . . "

"Beautiful," Jenny interrupted. "Tears my heart out. But you know something? You men are always more turned on by imaginary women than you are by the real thing. You get a real woman and when she doesn't fit into that nice neat little sonnet, you either try to change her or you dump her."

"That's a hell of a cynical thing to say."

"To paraphrase another poet, truth comes on little cynical feet."

At that point, a nervous, breakfast-bearing Lou emerged from the kitchen. "I could hear your voices all the way in there," she said. "Why can't you two try to get along?"

"Cause your benefactor's a prick," Jenny stated matter-of-factly.

Lou drew back the scrambled eggs.

"I'm sorry," Jenny groveled. "I take it back." Chastened, she sat silent. Lou didn't allow anyone to insult her darling.

Appeased, Lou set the food down in front of Jenny on the marble-topped coffee table, and Jenny began to eat happily away.

Ever the Good Woman, Lou fussed around Silver, brushing ashes off his trousers, straightening his collar. "Poor baby. You work so hard."

Jenny wasn't going to say another word until she had

finished off breakfast.

Silver basked in the attention. "Ah, sweetness." He patted Lou's plump arm. "Maybe I'll stay over again tonight."

Jenny couldn't stand it. "Hey. What about your wife? Isn't she going to get suspicious?"

Lou looked up at her in surprise. "Why, Jen. You know I'm not a sneaky person. Mrs. Silver knows all about me. And she approves, too. After all, men have different needs than women."

Silver nodded his head sagely. "That's right. Men are entirely different than women."

"Hah!" Jenny snorted. "Don't I know it? Let a man sleep around and he's called a stud, but let a woman do exactly the same thing and she's called a nympho or a neurotic."

Lou snatched the fork from underneath Jenny's mouth.

Jenny tried to be civil but it seemed that the hungrier she got, the meaner she got. She guessed that was how revolutions started. Someone got a little bit too hungry and couldn't take it any more. She knew she was hostile but she couldn't help it. Many was the day she would start off with good intentions, would say to herself, Jenny, this is *NICE* day. You're going to pat dogs on the head and smile at children. Today you're going to be nice. The all-American girl. If somebody asks you about Watergate you'll smile and say that all criminally accused should be considered innocent until proven guilty—instead of your usual "all those fucking mothers should be gelded." Judge not, Bretheren, you'll say. You will not cuss or pick your nose.

But Jenny wasn't a good girl. No matter what her original intentions, she always wound up giving the world the finger.

Lou hadn't cared to have her darling Sterling included in that gesture and had summarily thrown Jenny out of the apartment.

It was raining as Jenny trudged back to her studio and as she moved along Third Street she heard the sound of singing and chanting behind her. She turned and saw that she was being followed by a troop of white-robed, top-knotted teen-agers carrying incense under tiny umbrellas. "Hare Krishna. Hare Krishna. Hare, Hare, Hare," they sang to the accompaniment of clanging cymbals.

Jenny walked faster.

The group danced closer.

"Hare, Hare."

An anemic-looking girl ran up beside Jenny and said, "Hare Krishna."

"Hare Krishna," Jenny replied, as inoffensively as possible.

The girl was insistent. "Hare. Hare, Hare, Hare."

"Hare," Jenny said defensively.

"Hare Krishna!" the girl menaced.

Reinforcements moved up. Three more sandaled teen-agers threatened Jenny. "Hare, Hare!" they warned.

"Hare," Jenny surrendered and gave them her last thirty cents.

The girl smiled, said, "Peace be with you, Sister," and the group moved off.

The rain began to pour and Jenny stayed close to the building fronts, seeking protection. When she was only two blocks from her studio, the Pink Pussy came into sight, decorated conveniently with a pink and purple awning. Jenny took shelter gratefully, standing well away from the flashing neon sign Four Koy Kittens.

She seemed to be spending half her life under awnings, she thought glumly, in shelter from the rain, waiting for enchiladas to appear. Noticing the crudely painted picture of a dancing girl in a bikini on the building wall, Jenny shuddered. The artist was totally ignorant of human anatomy. The thighs on the girl were separated by a crotch area of at least six inches (which was a lot of pink pussy) and one waving arm emerged from the dancer's neck without the benefit of a shoulder. The girl's eyes were placed in the upper quarter of her head, leaving room for a brain no bigger than a fig. Probably intentional, Jenny thought.

A voice said mournfully, "Only three now."

Jenny turned to see a dully-handsome young man peering out the bar's door. She could hear music inside.

"Three?" she asked startled. "Three what's?"

The man pulled fretfully at his ruffled shirt. "Just three Koy Kittens left." He looked aggrieved. "Janice had a sex change operation, is now James and working as a sanitation engineer in Glendale."

Jenny shook her head in sympathy.

"I saw you from in there," he explained. "Any port in a storm, right?"

She laughed. "Right. I'll be moving along soon, though."

"Haste makes waste," he admonished. "Say. You're pretty as a picture. Maybe we could work something out."

"What do you mean?" He looked harmless but recent events made her doubt her judgment.

"Name's Lance Stone. I'm an actor, but right now I'm managing this place for my grandmother. Her arthritis is acting up." He held out his hand for Jenny to shake. She did, and let go fast.

"Cold hands, warm heart," he piped. "It's the energy crisis. I'm patriotic. Keep the thermostat inside at sixty-

46

five. Hell on the girls, though. They don't wear much. Still you reap what you sow. A girl goes in for topless dancing, she shouldn't complain about a goose bump here and there. Want a job?

Jenny was stunned. "Doing what?"

"Oh, just wearing a bikini and serving beer. The Pink Pussy is a nice place to work. We have Blue Cross, Blue Shield, we treat everybody right. My grandmother's very fussy about that. She's an ex-Ziegfield Girl. Runs a tight ship. The customers aren't rough; they're all nice although there may be one or two bad apples. Still, music hath charm to soothe the savage beast and there's almost never any trouble. How about it?"

"Well . . . uh."

"I know. You're cool. Cautious. Want to know the terms. Put your money where your mouth is, right? The pay is two seventy-five an hour plus all the tips you can scrounge—and believe me, they ain't hay. You might be able to get more elsewhere but I always say a bird in the hand is worth two in the bush. I'll only need you for Friday, Saturday, and Sunday nights. The hours are six to two. How's that?"

Jenny, suddenly seeing salvation staring her in the face, didn't hesitate. "Great. When do I start?"

"Tonight. Wear a bikini. And make-up. When in Rome, you know."

"Should I take a bath, too?" she asked dryly.

"Always better to be safe than sorry." He rubbed his chilled hands together. "Time I got back inside." His eyes slid to her outlined breasts. "That's not a silicone job, is it?"

Trying to hide her smile, Jenny replied, "No. I believe that honesty is the best policy."

He smiled broadly. "Right. You can't make a silk purse out of a sow's ear. A woman after my own heart. See you tonight. Don't take any wooden nickels!"

47

"Hi, Angela." Thirty minutes later Jenny stood at the door of Angela's and Sushi's neo-Nipponese apartment. "Where's the genius?"

"Getting the Ferrari fixed. What do you want?"

Angela knew Jenny well. Nonetheless, she invited her in and they both sat cross-legged on a grass mat.

Jenny, shameless, didn't even attempt a blush. "Oh, I just thought you might have a bikini I could borrow seeing as how you can't use one now. And maybe some make-up you've discarded since you became an earth mother."

Angela scowled. She spent a lot of time scowling lately. She was normally a tiny, delicate woman but was now swollen and irritable in the eighth month of pregnancy. She wasn't taking it gracefully.

Sushi had first spotted Angela hitchhiking down Sunset and had stopped to give her a ride on his Harley Davidson. She had told him that she had recently split from the Utah commune where she had been living for the past year because the men had passed a resolution making all the women jointly owned by the men.The men had pointed out that since they themselves had always been sexually available to all the women it was only fair that the women act likewise—whether they liked it or not. Angela had left on a matter of principle. Sushi—a sucker for a woman with principles (especially when decorated with a movie starlet face and big breasts)—invited her to crash at his place. And there she had remained for the past year, reclining on the straw mats, filleting his fish, and braising on his Wok.

Angela wasn't overly intelligent, but she was curious. "Gee. What do you want a bikini for? I thought you always skinny-dipped."

Jenny told all.

Angela giggled. "Oh wow. That's a gas. You of all

48

people!"

Jenny frowned. "Just what do you mean—me of all people?"

Angela kept giggling. "Oh, Jenny. It's not any secret that you despise men."

"I don't despise men." Hurt, and a little bit off balance, she tried to explain. "I just don't like them telling me what to do, that's all."

"Oh, admit, Jenny! You know how you are. All those one-night stands, never letting any one man stick around long enough for you to care for."

Angela's ingenuousness touched Jenny. "Angela, I wasn't born like this. Some things have happened to me along the way."

"Well. You know what I mean. Sometimes I've wondered if you were really a woman at all. You're more like a—what do they call it—a caricature."

Tears filled Jenny's eyes and she looked away.

Flustered, Angela rattled on. "Oh my. I've done it now! Gee. Sometimes I just talk before I think. I'm sorry, Jenny. I always seem to be putting my foot in my mouth."

"Don't worry about it," Jenny said quietly. "Can I borrow that suit?"

"Oh, sure." Angela waddled off into the bedroom and returned moments later with a macrame bikini. "Made it myself," she said proudly. "Terrific, isn't it?"

"Yes." Jenny's voice was faint.

Angela looked at her worriedly. "Jenny? I am sorry, honest. I know that I have no right in criticizing you but it's just that I'm a man's woman and it's hard for me to understand someone like you."

Jenny forced a smile. "A man's woman? Most women who use that expression just mean that they don't like other women."

Angela looked shocked. "Like women? Of course I

don't, Jenny! Gee. I'm no lesbian!"

Jenny sighed. "I'm sure you're very normal.
Where are you having the baby?"

Angela brightened. "Cedars. Sushi said nothing but
the best for his Angela. Private room and a nurse
when I come home. Did he tell you that we have been
taking natural childbirth classes together? He's actually
going to be with me when the baby is born!"

It was Jenny's turn to laugh. "Sushi? In a delivery
room? Ha!" She remembered the day that Sushi and
she had been walking in the door of Howard's Art
Supply when they had seen a freshly-killed dog
sprawled in the gutter. Whatever hit it had been big.
One eye hung upon its cheek, its teeth were scattered
for yards, and its belly was ripped open. Jenny had
bent over it, noticing the iridescent blue intestine lying
diagonally across a red pool of blood. Nice, she had
thought. I may be able to do something with that—
the color, the line. Very nice.

She had turned to find Sushi vomiting into the litter
basket, splattering the motto Keep Your City Clean.

Angela noticed Jenny's skeptical face. "He's getting
better, Jenny. Last week we saw a film of a woman giving birth and when it showed the doctor giving the
episiotomy, Sushi didn't even faint."

"Good luck with him. I've got a feeling you're
going to need it."

"Oh, I'm an Aries. We always think positively." Angela grew serious. "But we think ahead, too. I mean,
we are responsible people. Like, lately I've been thinking about my life with Sushi. Him being an artist and
all."

"What do you mean?"

"I'm beginning to think that a child needs a stable
father figure. Sushi's nice and all that, but you'll have
to admit that he isn't exactly dependable. My mother

50

always wanted me to marry someone with a sense of responsibility, like a doctor or a lawyer. And I'm beginning to think she's right."

"My, my. What has happened to the sweet, unspoiled flower child we all used to know and love?"

Angela looked important. "Maybe I'm growing up."

Jenny smiled. "Is that what you call it?"

Never able to keep her mind on one subject very long, Angela switched with lightning speed. "Do you think I'll get my figure back? In *Gone With the Wind* Scarlett O'Hara gained an inch on her waist after she had a baby."

"I wouldn't know. Pregnancy isn't my field."

"But certainly you plan on having a baby some day!"

"As a matter of fact, Angela, I'm not. Let others be fruitful is my motto. And besides, I'd really rather not discuss the state of my ovaries, thank you."

Angela giggled. "You're too much! Let's guess. What do you think it'll be?"

"Probably a girl or a boy."

"Oh, Jenny. You artists can't ever be serious! I'm hoping that it'll be a little girl. You can buy such cute clothes for them. I used to have this doll when I was a little girl. I had over twenty different outfits for her. More than anybody on my block. And then I got a boy doll, her boyfriend, and my mother made her the prettiest evening dresses! Just like a grown-up woman. One of them was even strapless!"

"Did your mother have the doctor fit the girl doll with a diaphragm, too?"

Angela made a noise something similar to "Awwkk!" Then she said, disapprovingly, "Be serious."

"I don't see what's so serious about a dating doll in a strapless evening dress."

"Well, if you must know, it prepares a girl for motherhood."

Jenny's eyes slid to the swollen, bulging belly. "I guess you've got something there."

They talked for a few minutes more, Angela showing Jenny some Lamaze breathing techniques her natural childbirth instructor had recommended. Jenny watched with interest, finding one of the positions (Angela lying on her back, belly protruding mountainously) oddly attractive. She committed it to memory. A painting, perhaps.

Angela told her about the movies Sushi had taken her to, the maternity clothes he had bought her, his consideration (when he remembered that she was around). She enthused, "Oh, Jenny. Gee. It's nice to be able to have a woman to woman talk, for a change!"

Jenny smiled and remembered something that had happened when she was thirteen. "Now that you're a woman," her mother had said as she handed Jenny a gauzy white Kotex, "there are some things we should talk about. One, never sit with your legs apart. Always keep your knees together. Two, never run. It makes your dress fly up. Three, sit up straight. It will make your breasts stick out."

Jenny agreed to these rules of conduct. Then her mother said, "There. Isn't it nice now that we can start having these woman to woman talks?"

Angela was blissfully unaware of that comparison. "Before you go, Jenny, Sushi wanted to know if the brochures for your exhibit have been printed yet. He'll scatter a few around for you."

"I'll make sure he gets them. I need all the help I can get."

At six on the dot, Jenny stood nervously in front of the

Pink Pussy, watching the Girls, Girls, Girls sign blink on
and off. Underneath her levis and shirt she was wearing the bathing suit Angela had lent her; it itched. Macrame, indeed! To make her even more miserable, the
make-up made her face feel stiff and greasy. "Well, coward, go on in," she told herself. "Two seventy-five an
hour is two seventy-five a fuckin' hour. That'll buy five
tacos, three Tommy Burgers, a giant bottle of Spanada,
six joints, two tubes of burnt sienna." With these visions
of luxury dancing in her head, Jenny steeled herself and
pushed open the door.

The smell of beer rushed out to greet her and fast
after it chased the bumping vibes of a jukebox. She
could hear voices and laughter.

With the up-yours air of Anne Boleyn at the chopping
block, she entered the bar and promptly banged into a
chair. Except for the lit stage, the Pink Pussy was pitch
dark; Jenny couldn't even see across the room. "Mr
Stone?" she called out.

"Lance," boomed a voice in her left ear.

She jumped, startled. "I can hear you but I can't see
you."

Laughter. "You'll get used to it in a minute. Come on.
I'll lead you to the dressing room and you can get out of
your civvies." A hand gripped her and propelled her forward. "This way."

They went through a curtain and into a lit room.

"Let there be light!" Lance chirped merrily.

Jenny stood blinking her eyes. "Well, soon as you're
ready to go out onto the floor, I'll show you the ropes."
He left the dressing room decorously, although Jenny
had half expected him to stay and watch. She looked
around. The dressing room was plain, but neat. The
walls were white and clean. The make-up stand and
mirror were free from dust or fingerprints—the tiny
room was unremarkable except for a giant poster of

Golda Meir on the back of the door. Underneath was lettered the words, But Can She Type?

Jenny chuckled and started to undress.

It was odd, how naked she suddenly felt. How vulnerable. She, the same Jenny West who could skinny dip in a crowd without one corpuscle expanding into a blush, was now horrified at her state of semi-undress.

As nervous as a virgin entering her first motel room, Jenny opened the door. Fortunately, Lance had waited for her, a faithful seeing-eye dog. "Right on!" he said. "Tough!"

"Thanks," she muttered, squinting her eyes. Her vision seemed to be getting better and she could dimly make out the ghostly outline of the bar against the far wall. Tables were beginning to emerge from the gloom, and human forms were starting to take shape. "I think my eyes are getting used to the light," she said.

"Great. Let's get started."

The bar was placed at the very back of the large, rectangular room. There was a shelf behind it which held an assortment of glasses, nuts, pretzels, potato chips, and gum. "Where's all the booze?" Jenny asked, looking around.

Lance raised his eyebrows. "This is a beer bar. Fifteen kinds of bottled beer, two on tap."

Jenny looked at the spigots. "Oh."

"That's really all you have to do," Lance explained. "Just pour the beer and wash the glasses. And wipe the tables and clean the ashtrays."

"That's it?"

"Well, when you get bored, you can shine up the fixtures on the bar. Wax the wood panel back there. The devil finds work for idle hands."

Jenny felt a little more confident. "Doesn't sound too complicated."

Lance laughed. "It isn't. But you have to be polite to

the customers."

Jenny's eyes were now entirely accustomed to the gloom and she looked around. The room was softly lit in pink, carpeted in a deep rose, and the chairs looked comfortable. At the far end of the room was the dancer's platform. It was raised to table level and lit with strobe lights which gave the performing dancer a mechanical, jerky appearance. Jenny guessed that it also served to hide whatever anatomical defects the dancer had.

"How long does she have to dance?" Jenny asked.

"Just for half an hour, then she gets a half-hour break. That goes on for four hours, till ten. Then another dancer replaces her. Well, I'll leave you for now and let you get started. Prices are on that pad next to the cash register. I'll be in the office—there's a button under the bar there in case you need me. Just buzz and I'll come running." He walked off leaving her on her own.

There were only two customers at the bar and three sitting at tables near the dancers. All had full glasses of beer. Jenny searched her mind to remember what barmaids acted like, found a suitable image from her art school days. She straightened her shoulders, walked over to the nearest customer, and said, "Everything all right, sir?"

He looked up at her. "Right on." He was about fifty, balding, and wore a gray suit with an American flag pinned in the lapel.

Jenny blinked and moved on to the next middle-aged customer. Here, too, she was told that everything was right on. Shrugging, she retreated to the far end of the bar and began to polish the wood panel.

Time went by quickly. Customers would signal her by waving their empty glasses and Jenny soon learned that the customers only wanted conversation when the dancer took a break. There were some Straights and Swingers there—Jenny recognized them from the laundromat; they were cheerful, aggressively hip; there were some older, more resigned men in business suits and a few obvious members of the lunatic fringe. These last lurked in the dark corner on the other side of the room. Jenny avoided it.

She soon learned to concentrate her attentions on the older men. They tipped well and usually tried to be polite. The younger men obviously thought that merely being in the vicinity of their handsome selves was largess enough. The businessmen tended to all look alike and they sounded alike, too, as they told Jenny their respective life stories.

They were all divorced, they said, after finding their wives in bed with their best friends (or insurance salesmen, or Sparkletts salesmen, according to the teller), had all suffered football injuries in the big game back at college (that was why they were in a topless bar instead of out dancing) and, yes, they were all broadminded men (they didn't forget to chuckle after "broad").

But what the hell, Jenny thought. They tipped well.

As the evening wore on and the glasses were refilled, the stories got better.

"Jewish women all have to be virgins when they marry or their father executes them with a ceremonial knife made of gold. The rabbi tests the girls in front of the whole congregation with a ceremonial phallus and if they bleed into a wine glass they're all right."

"Jack Ruby was injected with live cancer cells by a communist doctor who didn't want him telling that the whole assassination plot was communistic. Kennedy, see, was messing around with Kruschev's wife (no accounting for tastes, is there? Those liberals are sick)."

And, of course, "Those women libbers! All they really need is a good screw. Sex problems, that's their trouble. All that talk about equality. You show me a woman who talks like that and I'll show you a frigid dame!"

Bar maid. Jenny loved the word. It had such a raunchy earthy sound, like truck driver. Maybe it was the women's equivalent. The work itself was harder than she had imagined. Within forty minutes her feet hurt, her shoulders were sore from leaning over the tables with heavy steins of beer—in fact, there wasn't a part of her body that wasn't aching in some way. She was walking stiffly in Angela's platform shoes and after seeing herself, bikinied and painted in the dancers' mirror, Jenny came to the gloomy conclusion that she looked like a female impersonator.

Fashion, she decided, was absurd. Especially when it came to a woman's feet. Her movements were so hampered that she could barely mince across the carpet. Oh, they made her look long-legged and alluring all right, but they fixed her so she couldn't outrun a one-legged rapist.

Jenny remembered a story she had once read about a time in the future when a law had been passed in order to force all humans to practice perfect equality. The beautiful were made to wear hideous masks, the intelligent to wear ear phones which interrupted any thought with ringing bells, and the fleet and graceful had to drag around weights attached to various parts of their body. The world today hadn't gone that far—the more extreme measures were still confined to women. Her platform shoes, for instance.

The dancers were not so encumbered. They were barefoot. One came up to introduce herself during a break. Wanda Orlando (real name Shirley Tankersley) was a tall, dumb-looking blond who had a master's degree in political science at Cal State. She was presently working on her doctorate, she said. Her master's thesis—on the power of pressure groups in constitutional law—had actually been published, but royalties had been non-existent. "People don't seem to read that sort of thing," she mourned. She had found it necessary to supplement her daytime job as a typist for an insurance agency—it just didn't pay well enough to finance rent, food, tuition, and research.

Wanda wiped the sweat from under her pendulous breasts with a white bar towel. "Janine," she said, referring to the other dancer, who hadn't made her appearance yet, "is a housewife. Married to an advertising executive. Says she needed more glamour in her life." She looked pensive for a moment, then added, "Sure seems to be a lot of those around lately." She shook the dampness out of her long hair. "Oh well, back to the bump and grindstone."

She climbed up on the platform and began dancing to "Hide Your Love."

Lance emerged later that night from his office in back. He wanted to see how she was doing, he said, but it soon became obvious to Jenny that he merely wanted company. Jenny had found that handsome men like Lance had a tendency to wilt without an audience.

He chattered away, capped teeth flashing. "I've got a lot more going on upstairs than you think. Can't judge a book by its cover, you know. I've got a degree from UCLA in engineering—that's what I was going to be—but I soon found out that it wasn't my cup of tea. I'm a very creative person, you see. None of the nine to five for me, slaving away to bring home the bacon. No sirree. Not old Lance. So I quit my job at the office and tried to find myself. I knew that grass usually looks greener on the other side of the fence, of course, but God helps those who help themselves, I say. Nothing ventured, nothing gained. After much introspection (and some analysis at fifty bucks a shot, for Pete's sake) I decided to become an actor."

"Birds of a feather flock together," muttered Jenny.

"What's that? Oh, right! You obviously have an eye for beauty. Now I don't want to seem to be bragging, but my left side here is absolutely perfect. Not a flaw on it. See? I've had several cameramen compliment me on it. I've been in eight pictures so far. To be truthful, they were just walk-on parts, but I'm getting my foot through the door. I'm starting to attract favorable attention in the industry. I'll tell you, no grass is growing under my feet. I'm out there every day at the casting departments, the big agents. It's only a matter of time."

"Lance, I haven't the slightest doubt that you'll go right to the top. I can feel it in my bones."

"Right on, girl!" Lance's face lit up. "You're really a winner, you know? My kind of girl."

At closing time, which came surprisingly soon, he helped her clean up, washing the glasses and ashtrays, rubbing the bar to bowling-lane slickness. "Got to keep the place shipshape for Grandma," he explained. "She gets back from the nursing home, sees I've let the place go, she'll throw me out on my ear. Lots of sass left in that old gray mare!" He whistled "Up the Lazy River" as he worked.

When they were finished, he asked, "Need a lift home?"

"Well, I only live two blocks from here," Jenny said. "But I would appreciate it. I've been a little nervous lately."

"Smart girl. Fools rush in where angels fear to tread."

He dropped her off in front of her studio then roared off toward the San Fernando Valley in his orange Porsche. When Jenny opened the door, she saw a note attached to a copy of *Mosaic Life.*

Dearest Jenny,

I know you didn't mean all those things that you said. It's all right. Life has put us all under a strain. You're forgiven. Since you weren't here, I'm slipping this under the door for you. You'll love the magazine. My mother says you can keep it. I'll stop by and see you tomorrow.

All my love,
Brian

Jenny threw the note (along with *Mosaic Life*) into the garbage and went to bed.

She got up promptly at eight, a little stiff, but ready to work. The white canvas stared at her accusingly. It rose six feet high, demanding blood. Beginning a painting—getting that first stroke down on that grim purity—was always like this. It was like losing your virginity all over again—it began with high expectations and ended with disappointment.

How conceited, how pompous to think that she had the right to paint. Or as her mother had put it, "Just what makes you think you're so special, Miss Artsy-Craftsy? Always walking around thinking you were meant for better things!"

Her mother had a point. The sable hair brush had it all over the self-cleaning mop.

She primed with flat, wide strokes, stepping back from time to time to survey her canvas. She never primed evenly, preferring to leave some bare spots on foreground areas for flash. Beginnings were when you could get a good idea of the painting's chance for success or failure. Jenny thought this one might make it; it was beginning to sparkle already.

She was painting in acrylic this time. Oil was a purgatory, but acrylic could be hell. She had to work quickly, not letting the brushes dry with paint on them, keeping them in large pots of water and special cleaner the minute she set them down. The constant speed she had to keep up actually called for physical strength and endurance. It was a race; would the paint dry before she finished the stroke?

It was taking shape. Bright and raw this time—no grays on the palette. It would show a contorted Wanda Orlando reflected into infinity in her dancer's mirror. *Breasts* she would call it. Jenny smiled, thinking what a powerful exhibition hers would be—deserving of a write-up in the art columns.

As she began blocking out the foreground, she heard a knock at the door. She yelled, "Piss off!"

But the knocking didn't stop. It rose to an insistent banging. Jenny threw down her paint rag, put her brush down, and went to the door.

Standing there was Brian Hampshire-Landrace, bearing bonbons and breathing heavy.

Jenny was furious. "I'm busy! Bug off!"

"Sweets for the sweet," he said with a Great Dane smile. "I told you I'd be by today."

"Telling and getting are two different things," Jenny tried to shut the door. "Get lost. I have work to do."

He got his foot in the door. "You try to act so hard all the time," he cooed. "You're just trying to cover up feelings of insecurity. I see it all the time with my minority students. Don't worry, I understand."

Jenny was exasperated. "Look. My insecurities are my own business. What you're forgetting is that this is the day of casual sex. Ships that pass in the night and all that shit. We don't marry everybody we go to bed with and we don't even have to see them again, either. This whole scene just kills me. For years you men complained that women confused love with sex. Now that we don't anymore, all you do is sit around and whine about that! I wish you characters would make up your fucking minds what you want! Now I don't want to hurt your feelings—you were great, I came three times—but I can't

61

spend my life murmuring sweet nothings to you. I'm busy with other things."

He looked puzzled. "Busy with what? From what I can see, all you're doing is painting!"

"Get the fuck out!"

Brian was digging in and behind him, on the sidewalk, a crowd was forming. Jenny heard one man say to another, "This is the greatest place! I've seen her throw as many as three people out in one day!" A woman was passing around peanuts.

Brian said, "I'm not leaving. I've found the girl of my dreams and I'm not going to stand by and see her throw herself away on some silly hobby. With a little help you could be a fine wife and mother."

Someone in the crowd took a poll: would the redhead make a good wife and mother? Fifteen percent of the women thought she would. Eighty-five percent of the men thought she would.

Brian continued, "By the way you made love I could tell that you have a fine, warm heart. You've just had some bad experiences and are afraid of showing your feelings."

"My God! Do you really think you can tell anything about a person from the way they screw? I'm just a horny type, that's all. In case you haven't noticed, my heart and my hole aren't located in the same place."

The crowd gasped and the poll was renewed. One hundred percent of the men now had great hopes for her.

Brian looked scandalized. "Jenny, sweetheart. You shouldn't talk like that!"

Jenny ran back into her studio and picked up a metal T-square. She came to the door, swinging.

Brian fled. The crowd scattered except for one man in a gray suit, carrying an avocado briefcase. "I love you. Will you marry me?" he asked Jenny.

"Piss off!" Jenny screamed, and swung.

He ran off after Brian.

She went back into her studio. The paint was dry on her brush. Cursing, she tried to salvage it.

At five, exhausted, irritated, and depressed, she began getting ready for work. "Insane," she muttered. "Lunatic." She was ready to go to bed and sleep, but there she was, painting her face and donning a macrame bathing suit—the better to entertain the customers with. "Nuts." She looked blearily at the emerging painting and wondered if she would ever be able to finish it. Arthritis seemed to be settling in her right shoulder.

"Lord, please Lord. Let it be slow tonight!"

But when she got to the Pink Pussy, she found that the crowd had doubled from the night before. Lance met her at the door, excited, nearly dancing with delight. "Jenny girl. You're a hit!"

Jenny looked at all the men waiting with empty glasses and expectant faces and groaned. Lance babbled happily, "Grandma will be so happy! She always said I couldn't pick them. This will show her!"

"Just goes to show you, then. Still waters run deep," Jenny muttered. She trudged off to the dressing room to discard her clothes. Wanda winked as she passed the dancer's platform.

The night passed more slowly than the night before—probably because Jenny was moving more slowly. Her feet were swollen and sore, and her right shoulder had stiffened into near-immobility. The customers' faces and stories blurred together and by closing time Jenny realized that she couldn't recall half the night. She had wandered the floor in a daze, filling glasses, wiping ashtrays, muttering mechanically, "Sorry, I don't date customers." When Lance dropped her off at the studio, she fell into bed with her clothes on, saying weakly, "Ah shit."

The next day she didn't paint. She sat on her mattress, wrapped in a blanket, feeling her muscles lock up. From time to time she groaned. She tried to tell herself that the experience would be good for her. After all, her life had so far, by necessity, been a lonely one. As one of her teachers had told her, "No great painting was ever done by a committee—so go home alone and paint!" Jenny had done just that for years, and had grown almost totally isolated from the civilization around her. The Pink Pussy promised to bring her back in touch; it would be a crash course in the human condition.

She guessed she could despise everyone down there if she had wanted to. After all, that dark roaring place reduced them all—including herself— to stereotypes. Ego trippers. Drunks. Escapists. Conformists with that fear of uniqueness so common, so prevalent in Southern California. But sitting there on her mattress, Jenny just shrugged her tired shoulders. Not for her to condemn that frenzied huddling together. Society loved to piss on a loner.

They all seemed to be so terrified of being alone. That was why the Pink Pussy was doing such a thriving business. It wasn't really the dancers, they just gave those men a socially-accepted reason to huddle together. Instead of frightened, lonely men, the dancer changed them into wise-cracking rogues. She performed a social service.

Jenny looked around her studio. Her paintings were all stacked together, waiting for Pearce to truck them away to his gallery. "You should be finished now," he had muttered the last time she saw him. "I don't like this last minute business. After all, I've consented to hold my gallery open for you for an entire month. The least you can do is have everything all finished and delivered well in advance."

Jenny nodded to herself. She had to agree. The trouble was finishing. There was *Breasts* sitting up there on the easel and here she was squatting down on the mattress, too exhausted to move. And she needed another painting. Preferably a large one.

She groaned and rested her head on her knees.

That night the crowd was even bigger. "Did you expect them to be in church?" Lance giggled as Jenny displayed surprise. "Sunday's our biggest night."

Jenny dragged herself slowly into the dressing room past a sympathetic-looking Wanda Orlando. Lance followed Jenny. "There's a guy been in here looking for you," he explained. "Real weird type. You in trouble?"

Jenny, puzzled, shook her head. "Not that I know of."

Lance motioned out the door. "That's him over there at the corner of the bar."

Jenny stuck her head out of the door and saw Brian Hampshire-Landrace sitting at the bar. "Aw shit," she said. "Holy, mother-fucking shit!"

Lance squeaked in distress. "Now, that's not nice. Don't let the customers hear you talk like that. The Pink Pussy has an image to uphold."

Jenny started to reply, then changed her mind. Two seventy-five an hour was two seventy-five an hour. "Sorry," she said, and began to pull off her T-shirt.

"Oh, let me get out first," said Lance. "Grandma doesn't like me to be in the dressing room when the girls are getting ready. Out of sight, out of mind." He shot out the door.

Jenny braced herself and went to the bar where an outraged Brian waited.

"I thought I saw you come in here yesterday," he said, aggrieved, "but I just couldn't believe it. I thought

65

you had more taste. More class. But here you are, lowering yourself just like all the rest of them." He waved an airy hand, indicating Lance, Wanda, et al. "This is no place for you to be working," he hissed. "I'll bet every man in here is thinking just one thing about you."

"They're probably right, too," she called over her shoulder as she passed.

He wouldn't tip her although he kept her scurrying back and forth for napkins, peanuts, salt, beer. "It wouldn't be appropriate, considering," he explained as he had her wipe his table for the fifth time. The pride of ownership gleamed in his eyes.

"Considering what?" she said between clenched teeth.

"Considering our relationship."

Jenny digested that in silence.

"Sweetheart, a friend of mine works in a law office and he needs a receptionist. He'll give you the job."

"I don't want to be a receptionist. And stop discussing me with your friends."

"I don't talk about . . . *that*. And besides, what's wrong with being a receptionist? At least it's respectable. People are liable to get the wrong idea about you with your working here."

"Oh shit. I don't care what kind of ideas they get, just as long as they tip well. Don't you realize that if I worked a day job I'd only be able to paint in the evenings. That is, if I wasn't too tired when I came from work."

"Honey, it's all right to have a hobby. I'm all for that. But it's getting out of hand with you. You need more balance in your life."

Jenny's tombstone rose up in front of her. Here Lies Jenny West. She Had Balance.

"I don't want to have balance. What's so great about that? A little of this, a little of that, a pinch of this, a smidgen of that. It's like a goddamn recipe for ginger-snaps. If that's how you want to live your life, well boogie on ahead, but leave me out of it. You can't get good at one thing if you're trying to do too many others."

Brian smiled. "You'll eventually see it my way."

"Look, I don't want you in here again."

He looked pained. "Why not? This way I can help make sure nothing happens to you."

"Brian, has it occurred to you that I like having things happen to me? Front-porch-swing security is for other people, not me. And besides, I'm getting sick and tired of your criticizing the way I live."

"It's my right," he explained. "I love you."

So there it was. In the end, it always came to that. When they loved you, they wanted to change you. They felt love gave them the right to tell you how misdirected you were, how selfish, how misguided. Love meant open season on your psyche.

"Don't tell me you love me," Jenny snapped. "All do is disapprove of me."

"Jenny, baby. I don't disapprove of you. Just of the way you live."

"Has it occurred to you that they're one and the same?"

"Oh, no. The real Jenny West is a sweet, loving girl. You're just going through a phase, that's all."

"Brian. Get the fuck out of my life."

He looked stunned. "You can't mean that! Why, I want to marry you!"

Slowly, clearly, and with malice aforethought she said to him, "I do not love you. I do not even like you. You screw like a sheep. Your mother sucks."

He got up, slapped her hard on the face, and left.

Lance, who had been hovering discreetly in the corner, hurried over. "Wow, Jenny. You sure get along with the customers. What happened?"

Jenny pressed the cool bar rag to her flaming cheek. "The wages of sin," she muttered.

He looked at her sympathetically. "Oh well. No use crying over spilt milk."

Later, Lance retreated to his office. "Gonna do some bookwork," he explained. Jenny knew that meant he was going to take a nap.

She stood, bored and irritable, at the bar, her cheek beginning to cool. It had been painful, but she guessed that she had seen the last of Brian. She mentally apologized to his mother—a pawn in the battlefield.

The crowd thinned early that night, in deference to blue Monday; at midnight, Jenny had only one customer left. He was hunched in the corner, a big forbidding young Black in a leather jacket, dark glasses, and a huge exploding afro. Not a type she especially cared for but at least a respite from the token Toms.

He snapped his fingers, indicating his need for attention. "Another beer?" she asked.

"Yeah."

She got him a tall, cold draft and walked over to the table with it. 'That'll be one dollar."

"Put it on my tab, Mama," he said.

"We don't run tabs here, Daddy." She didn't like customers to act familiar even if they had been discriminated against for two hundred years. She figured she was a few thousand up on them.

She saw a flash of white behind his shades.

"Uppity, aren't you?" he asked.

"Takes one to know one." She took the twenty dollar bill he put down.

More white. "WOOOOEEEE! You prejudice, honey or just nasty?"

She didn't answer and went to the register to get his change. Banter wasn't really her style, but she was so

68

bored she'd do anything for a little lively conversation.
It beat talking about Hank Aaron. When she returned
with his change, he was smiling and the shades were off.
The better to see her with, no doubt.

He began the standard friendly noises. "Live around
here?"

"Why? You going to follow me home?"

His smile broadened. "I don't make it with white
chicks, baby. Just making conversation."

"How bourgeois."

She had hit the magic button. He jammed his shades
back on and snarled, "You gonna wake up some day
without a head, honky chick!"

Jenny grinned. "Oh boy! A real, live radical! Can I
have your autograph? An empty cartridge for a sou-
venier?"

For a moment it looked like she was about to get
her second slap of the night, but his snarl swiftly
changed to a grin. "Sure are a feisty fox, ain't ya?"

She smiled back. "No, I just have a well-developed
death wish."

His smile grew brilliant. "Well, well. The fox reads.
Maybe even has an ed-u-ca-tion." He strung it out. "Tell
me," he leered. "What's a nice girl like you doing in a
place like this?"

"Just waiting for my chauffered Rolls to pick me
up."

They both laughed, and he said, "I'll move my stuff
closer to the bar so you don't have to run so far back
and forth."

He bought her a beer. (Lance allowed a maximum of
four a night. "But no more. Can't have our gals getting
tipsy, right? Might start making the wrong change. You
know what I always say—a fool and his money are soon
parted.")

He introduced himself; his name was Mohammed

Imara, but she could call him Mo. And he wasn't really a revolutionary. In fact, he embarrasedly informed her, he had actually voted for Richard Nixon. They both digested this confession in silence. But he wasn't an Uncle Tom, either, he said. He had absolutely no plans on going to work for the post office.

"So what are you?" she asked. "A nuclear physicist?"

"I'm a writer," he said. His street talk had vanished.

Jenny was suitably impressed. "What do you write?"

"Pornography," he grinned. "And children's books."

The doubt showed in Jenny's face.

"Would I lie to a nasty bitch like you?" he asked.

Jenny laughed. "I guess not. But I don't get it. How can one person possibly write both? They seem worlds apart."

"Nope. Not at all. They have a lot in common. They're both fantasy; they both appeal to about the same age level. I get ideas for the kids' books while I'm writing the porn and vice versa. About the only difference is that with the kids' books you have to have a good solid plot or the kids don't go for it. They're a little more sophisticated, I think. Plot is only incidental with porn."

"But if plot is incidental, how do you write? I don't understand."

"Oh, simple. I have a big stack of three by five cards with one perversion written on each. Then I shuffle them up, deal me a hand of twenty, and write away."

"Can I ask you a personal question?"

"Why, sure."

"Are you a pervert?"

He roared with laughter. "Fox, I'm depressingly straight. I get most of my perversions out of the L.A. County Library."

Mo went on to tell her that he had had three children's books published and seven porn novels. He had been writing for three years, he explained, and could dash off a porn in three or four weeks but had to spend quite a bit of time on the kids' stuff. "The kids are more discriminating." He told her his titles:

The Lord Saved Her When The Preacher Laid Her.
Forty-Six D and Hungry.
Jimmy and the Wonderful, Magical Giraffe.
Whips, Spurs, and Long Black Boots.
Friday Night at the Zoo. ("Porn, that one.")
Lulu Goes to Town. ("Kids' book.")
The Dyke Before Christmas. ("My best seller—a holiday special.")
The Pink Pony.
And *Around the World in Eighty Ways.*

Jenny was impressed. "You sound successful."

"No." He shook his head. "Doesn't pay worth shit. I have to work in my old man's factory to get enough bread to live on."

"A factory? What kind of factory?"

"A rosary factory. My dad manufactures rosaries."

Mo flashed his big white teeth and laughed; Jenny laughed in amazement with him. They chatted until Janine went off the stage, signalling that it was one-thirty, and almost time to close up. Mo sighed and gathered up his change. "Well, I'll be pushing off, Fox. Okay if I drop in again? Talk?"

Jenny nodded. "And bring some of your stuff."

"Which?"

Jenny laughed. "Both."

Mo grinned and left.

"Let's get out of here," Lance shouted from the bar where he was washing glasses. "I've got somebody to visit. All work and no play makes Lance a dull boy." The water gurgled as he pulled the plug in the sink. "And by the way, here's your paycheck."

Jenny grabbed it gratefully.

"Don't spend it all in one place," Lance admonished as she ran off into the dressing room. "Save some for a rainy day!"

Monday. She was in the chips again and finally she could pick up some badly-needed art supplies. Howard's was only three blocks away, a large, block-long store which specialized in artist's materials for the professional.

Bert saw her first. "Oh, Jenny. I've been hoping you'd come in. Wait until you see what we just got." Bert was an artist himself—tall, thin, fuzzy-haired, creative in bed, too. Jenny had slept with him several times but stopped when he started making derogatory comments about her work. He hadn't been able to handle the fact that she was a more accomplished artist than he, a not too uncommon problem when two artists made it together. Almost always, one of them wound up cleaning the brushes of the other.

Jenny bore no grudges and neither did Bert. She preferred him as a salesman since he knew in what direction her work was headed.

Excited, he led her to a new display rack. "Just look at these! A whole new line of acrylics, pre-mixed tints and shades. Aren't they great? Look at the brilliance! I tried some of them and I swear it looked like I had added da-glo to the pigment. This stuff is selling like crazy to the illustrators."

She picked and poked, opened tubes to compare the color inside with the charts, and found six new colors she thought she would try.

"Now you're sure they will mix with my other acrylics. No undissolved flecks?"

"Oh, I swear to the great god Dali," said Bert.

"They're guaranteed." He patted her fanny in a friendly way and turned to another customer.

Jenny looked for a while at the glossy, expensively-bound art books, running her fingers over the smooth pages, comparing the reproductions with the originals she remembered at the County Museum. Printing seemed to be improving. Back in art school, one of her teachers had shown her four different reproductions of the Mona Lisa; it was as if the same painting had been done in four different color schemes. The only way to see what Mona really looked like, was to visit the Louvre.

Leaving the prohibitively priced books, she went back to the paint rack and picked up nine tubes of her regular brand in her most frequently used colors: cobalt blue, chrome yellow, yellow ochre, raw umber, and others. She also got a giant jar of gloss medium for her glazes. As she was dumping the tubes into a cart, she was tapped on the arm and a deep voice said, "Excuse me, Miss, but I need some help and you look like you know what you're doing."

He was tall, trim, and either sold insurance or worked for IBM. He wore an American flag in the lapel of his suit. Short-haired, squeaky clean.

"How can I help you?"

"Well, I'm a little confused here. I wanted to pick up a painting kit for my nephew's birthday—he's ten—but that fuzzy-haired thing over there keeps trying to sell me everything in the store. I may be ignorant but I'm not stupid.

Jenny smiled. An apt distinction. "Yeah. Bert gets paid a bonus when he sells over his quota. Come on, I'll take you to the beginner's kits."

She led him over to the hobby section which was as different from the rest of the store as was mink from a beaver. "Get a small one," she advised. "The fewer colors he has, the more he'll learn. He'll have to mix."

"Oh, thank you. Thank you very much." He found a small set of oils and picked out six brushes.

"And you'll need something for him to paint on, too. Get canvas board. The paint won't bleed through."

He smiled at her—a surprisingly pleasant, relaxed smile. Jenny felt the first small stirrings of sexual excitement. Oh, no, she thought. Not with Mr. America!

"You certainly seem to know a lot about painting. Are you an artist?"

She was silent for a moment. Give him the slightest encouragement and it would be all over. The executive type was short on time and subsequently moved fast.

"Yes. As a matter of fact, I am." She tilted her head slightly which she knew caused her long red hair to ripple across her shoulders. "But I don't think you would like my style."

"Oh, I'm sure I'd love your style." He looked like a cat hearing the splash of milk in a saucer.

Jenny smiled a grim smile. If she did this, she certainly had no shame. She heard herself answering, "Well, why don't you come over to my studio and see?"

The cat changed into a joyful puppy. "Great! My car's right outside. Let me pay for this stuff and we'll go." He paused, and added, "I'm actually very interested in art. I bought a big oil at a place called the Pearce Gallery. It's a big seascape and the orange sky matches my carpet perfectly."

"I'm sure it's lovely. I can tell you're a man of taste." She added silently to herself that it was too bad that her sense of taste was located between her legs.

Two hours later, Mr. America was gone. Super-efficient to the very end, he had "slam, bang, thank you maam'ed" her and whisked out the door leaving Jenny still on top of the mountain. She contemplated mastur-

74

bating, but instead she got up and dressed. She was hooked on the real thing.

Here it came. A cold turkey pickup. The hardest kind.

Picking up a man was easy enough—any fool could do it—but picking up one in such a way as to insure yourself a good fuck was a difficult task. First, there was the matter of etiquette. "Always let the man take the first step," Jenny's mother had told her, never realizing that her advice would be used for more than the following of dance partners. The problem was that all those men had been told the same thing by their mothers and if a woman became too obvious, too forward, the men responded with a lightning screw and disappeared into the wilderness, muttering "slut" out of the sides of their mouths.

You had to be cool.

Her mother also said, "Boys never respect a girl who lets them kiss her on the first date." Jenny interpreted this as meaning, "Don't let him squeeze your breast the first time he tries."

She sighed. Getting a little was getting harder and harder all the time, because now "meaningful relationships" were in vogue.

She plotted her course. Howard's was out. Bert wouldn't be speaking to her for a while after seeing her get into the car with Mr. America. And the park was out. Only the lonely and really desperate hung around there. She had learned from sad experience that there was always a damned good reason all those men up there were so hard up. She had sampled the menu twice. One had come equipped with an illustrated copy of the Kama Sutra and had insisted on trying five different positions during the same sex act. The last had been totally impotent, preferring to masturbate in front of the mirror on Jenny's medicine cabinet. He had to stand on the toilet seat to watch himself.

Something would turn up. Something always turned up when a woman had red hair.

Beverly Boulevard was fairly busy: Volkswagens were travelling east towards downtown; XKE's heading west towards Beverly Hills. Jenny decided to opt for a little class and turned west. Who knows, she might meet a horny millionaire with a passion for painting.

By the time she had travelled three blocks, she had had two offers—one from a drunk being thrown out of a bar and another from a geriatric case driving a DeSoto. Neither appealed to her. But there, standing on the corner of Western and Beverly, backpacked and bespectacled, was a likely prospect. A specimen of sun-set funk. On the front of his patched army jacket were sewn the words "Reagan Eats It."

Yes. A likely prospect but one which must be approached with the utmost caution. That type took fright easily.

Jenny sat down at the bus stop, crossing her slim legs demurely, and began to cast sidelong glances at him. He had been well trained and made the proper response, "What's happening, man?"

But, hard to get at all times, Jenny just batted her thick lashes, held her breath, and tried to blush. The compleat female. Her quarry moved closer, straightening his counter-culture slump. "Say, man, know where Vine Street is?"

Jenny smiled a timid little smile and looked confused. Women weren't supposed to know one direction from another. "Well, I'm not very good at giving directions," (she noticed an approving look on his face) "but I think it's somewhere over there." She pointed in the opposite direction.

The self-effacing approach never failed. The big strong man preened his beard. "I think it's the other way."

She batted some more. "You're probably right. I get

76

so confused about things like that."

Emboldened, he struck. "Say, how about a sunflower seed. Guaranteed organic."

Thanking him, she crunched delicately. "Oh, wonderful. Thank you so much. I really believe in the organic process."

Thus encouraged, he went for broke. "If you think those are good, you ought to try some of this." He flashed a baggie at her. "Smoke?"

She allowed a faint expression of alarm to cross her face. "Oh, I don't know if I should. I mean, I don't even know you."

He smiled a big, broad smile. "Name's Mickey. Mickey Bedner. I'm just traveling across this fucked-up country of ours, trying to get my head together, trying to find out where it's at."

She batted. "That's so profound. My name's Jenny."

He took her tiny hand into his own huge one and squeezed it warmly. "Where can we go to smoke?"

It was like taking candy from a baby. He followed her to her studio, admired the paintings (she was careful to tell him her old man did them) and, formalities over, they lit up.

He took care of her. Completely.

Once started it was hard to stop. After being a good girl and painting energetically for two more days she couldn't stand it any more and decided to go out and paint the town Venetian Red.

Armed with righteous hedonism, she took off for the Balls aynd Tyte—one of those sprouting pseudo-English singles pubs specializing in cock rock, where every Wednesday night was ladies' night. It was half-timbered and black-lighted. A real home away from home for the visiting limey group.

A new band was there, hardly distinguishable from the old one. They flaunted the standard and required amount of hair, uneven teeth, and tissue-stuffed crotch. Jenny shuddered. She had gone that route once. Snagging her prey, a drummer, had been easy. She had had only to drool the required number of drops and he had followed her home. But what a waste! Upon removing his cool, dark shades, she had found that his eyes were beady and red from too much doping, too much drugging. Peering closely at his cascading curls she had seen dandruff and a bald spot. He was somewhat less than magnificent in bed, too. He had wheezed asthmatically into her ear and climaxed after five seconds (she counted). Then, adding insult to injury, he had lit up a joint and smoked it all by himself.

They were spoiled, these musicians. Jenny experienced a surge of rage when she saw young girls, aspiring groupies, pandering to their disdain. They were making things worse, she knew. The musicians had gotten to the point where they were treating women as mere vessels to masturbate in. Even, or perhaps especially, the mighty were affected. There had been that peculiar epithet a Rolling Stone had shouted when he had learned that a co-performer might not be able to make a concert date. "He's a cunt!" the Stone had screeched. "A stupid, dirty cunt!" Odd, to think that the worst word he could think of was that very female organ he had sung so many paens of delight about.

So Jenny swore off musicians. Let them masturbate in someone else. She preferred a little reciprocation.

She shifted her weight, resting it upon her other hip for a while. Stan, the manager, had removed all the bar stools and had substituted a long brass rail. "More authentic," he had explained. Maybe—but it contributed

78

to the number of bodies on the floor after too many drinks. Jenny's would probably be added to them.

Stan tried to help her along, though. Before she got totally blind he would switch her, without comment, to straight tonic. And he could be counted on to call her a cab or to get her a ride home with someone safe. He figured he had a personal interest in Jenny's welfare; he owned one of her paintings.

"How goes it?" he asked.

"All right, I guess. I'm just about ready for the exhibit but I'm beginning to wear down."

"Ever try cutting down on your love life?"

"What love life? If it's balling you mean, I only do that between paintings." Stopped by the skeptical look on his face she added, "Most of the time."

He grinned.

"You heard about my job?"

Stan nodded, his face sympathetic.

"It's taking more out of me than I thought, but hell, I don't know what else I could do. I have to eat. What worries me is—what happens after the exhibit? Do I go through the whole thing all over again?"

Stan listened silently. He had heard it all before from her—she was notorious for sobbing on shoulders—but, being a friend, he didn't mind a little repetition. He patted her hand. "You're good, Jen. It'll work out."

Jenny leaned across the bar and kissed his cheek. Originality in praise was no more necessary than originality in complaint. With a final hand squeeze, Stan moved off to serve other customers.

Left alone, Jenny began to look around. Standing next to her was a tall young man right out of an art history book—the classical Greece chapter. An Adonis— slender, with long black hair and wide almond eyes. He wore low denim hip huggers and a brief top; she could see the black pubic hair which started an inch above his belt line. It was all she could do to keep her hand from snaking over to his belly.

She looked at him hopefully, hoping that he would see her flaming hair and straight nose, but he was either too stoned or too drunk to see further than the glass in his hand. She couldn't bring herself to say something and subsequently cursed her mother and Billy Graham for decreeing that it was not proper for young ladies to make advances to young men. Young ladies were supposed to wait until they were noticed—but how did that happen if the object of your affections couldn't see two feet in front of his nose?

Sweat broke out on Jenny's forehead as she inwardly screamed, "Look at me!" But he just kept staring into his beer, oblivious.

Stan came around and gave her another drink. No vodka, she noticed. The bitter tonic drew the roof of her mouth.

Maybe a dance.

Throwing pride and caution to the wind, she leaned toward Adonis and asked, "Do you dance?"

He stared at her, eyes unfocused. "No," he whispered softly, and returned to his glass.

Jenny decided to kill herself. She really would. She couldn't take the rejection.

But at that point, a jock cruised by, letter sweater and all, and hauled her off to the dance floor. The band was loud, fast, and danceable. The sound enveloped them and it seemed as if the whole world was concentrated right there on the tiny dance floor. Bodies sweated and glistened. As ever, the rhythm roused her spirit. Life was beautiful, after all. She would become the greatest artist that had ever lived. She would hang in the Louvre and when she died, people would march in the streets of Paris, carrying candles. In Los Angeles they would name a shopping center after her.

But the song was short and the band hurried off on break. Somebody turned the juke box up.

Her Adonis had been captured by a young girl in a sequinned sweater. She was rubbing her hand up and down the small of his back. A goner, Jenny felt sick.

"Stan. Can I have an alka-seltzer?"

"Sure thing, kid." He pushed one towards her.

The jock hung around until Jenny told him that she had had a rather unusual discharge for the last couple of days, then he took to his cordovan heels. Jenny smiled. That got rid of them every time.

What was that? The sequinned girl leaving with somebody else? Jenny looked at the end of the bar. The Adonis remained.

What could she do? "Please, God," she prayed. "If you're not dead and are still up there, I have a message from down here. Jenny West has tried to be a good girl. Honest Injun. I'm a backslider, I know, but if you make that pretty boy look my way just once then I swear I'll go to church next Sunday. Honest, God."

Maybe if she could think of something original to say. Something witty or profound. Something different. With a sense of horror she heard herself saying, "Come here often?"

Adonis stared at her as if she had just grown scales. At least she had woken him up. Then he turned and left.

Yes, Jenny decided that she would definitely kill herself. Just as soon as she finished *Breasts.*

The band went back on stage and Jenny saw Stan pouring vodka into her tonic. Maybe life was still beautiful. She noticed the shadows the dancers made against the wall. Interesting. Out of her pocket she took her ever-present sketch pad and made a few marks. Nothing was a total loss, she reasoned. A painting could come of this.

Paintings. And experiences.

One night she and Sushi had come in together. A man had approached them. "I'm having some people over to smoke," he said. "Want to come?"

Sushi—kamikaze to the core—had answered for them both. "Just give us the address, man."

At first, the party had looked standard: posters on the walls, Jethro Tull's "Passion Play" fluting from cassettes, a mixed crowd giggling and whispering. But with the appearance of the first roach clip, their host had announced, "Just wait here, folks. Got a little surprise."

Intrigued, Jenny and Sushi had waited. "Here," the man said, after returning from the bedroom. "Take a snort of this." He held out a Vicks nasal inhaler. Jenny sniffed.

The rocket lifted off and she was blasting around outer space, keeping up with the comets—playing tag with their tails. She was golden. Everything was beautiful—peace and love. Narcs were all such nice sweet men with families it was so silly to worry when they would love her just as much as she loved them and Jesus Christ was really a woman, too, and nobody should fight because she'd settle everything once she got down off this goddamn cross somebody had tacked her up on but it was okay because she knew she had greatness in her since it was jumping out of her fingertips like sparks lighting up the world so that they would all see her for what she was—the saviour of them all, suffer children and come unto me only not in my mouth because it makes me sick and my God, the rocket's landing here I am

I'm back.

Jenny looked around. A face leered at her. "How was that? Far out, right?"

Next to her Sushi was grinning vacantly at the ceiling but she managed to half push, half drag him out the door with her. Their host gave them the finger.

Sushi came down. "Holy shit, what was that?"

"I don't know, but I thought it was time we left. Moderation in all things and all that shit."

Sushi looked frightened. Artists preferred their dissipation in smaller doses.

That had been months before and the pusher no longer hung around the Ball aynd Tyte. Jenny hoped he was somewhere nice and safe like Folsom Prison.

Everybody was making breakfast dates. "Need a ride, Jen?" asked Stan as he washed glasses.

But Jenny saw, standing by the door, her Adonis, thumbs hooked in his belt loops. Whatever he had been taking had worn off. He was smiling at her.

"No thanks, Stan," she said. Here goes. Hold your nose and dive in.

"Hi," she said to Adonis.

"Hi." His lashes were an inch long. "I have a bike, if you need a ride."

Lochinvar and his steed.

"I'd love a ride, thanks." His smile broke her heart. Thank you, God.

"Where do you want to go?" he asked, more shyly than she would have expected him to.

"Anywhere," she answered. "But let's start at my place."

He was incredibly, heartbreakingly sweet. He undressed her slowly, stopping to ask every now and then—is this all right, am I hurting you—you're so beautiful—tell me what you want. He was peach colored and his hair was soft. She twirled it around her fingers, buried her face in it.

He made love gently, slowly, and at the climax whimpered softly. She cradled his head against her and stroked him. He fell asleep but she lay awake for hours, just holding him.

The next morning she told him to leave and not come

back. He embraced her silently at the door, and left.

Then Jenny sat on the floor and cried.

Later that day, as Jenny was starting to feel better and was working it all out on canvas, Wanda Orlando came by. Wanda looked with dismay at the brush in Jenny's hand. "Oh. I'm sorry. I didn't know you would be working."

"Just painting my troubles away," Jenny explained, "and to tell the truth, I'm glad to have the company. Come on in." She opened the door wide and Wanda entered the studio. "You sure look different," she cracked, "clothes on and no makeup." And it was true. Wanda no longer looked vacuous. Instead, she looked like an intelligent woman and, for the first time, Jenny could believe that Wanda indeed had written a dissertation on constitutional law. Jenny looked around the studio desperately, trying to find a place where she could (hostess-style) motion her guest to sit. "Pull up a stool or a mattress."

Wanda sat down on the mattress, tucking her long legs under her. "Nice to see someone who's gotten down to the bare essentials of life," she said with a smile.

Jenny put her brush in water and got a bottle of Spanada from the floor of the closet. She poured out two dixie cups full and they drank a toast to the bare essentials.

"So how do you like working at the Pink Pussy?" Wanda finally asked.

"Money's money," Jenny answered. "Lance may be a bore but at least he's not a letch."

"Only because he thinks you're a lesbian. Are you?"

Startled, Jenny almost dropped her dixie cup. "God, no!" she squeaked. "Jesus! What made him think that? Hell, I'm straight as a T-square."

"I guess he thought that because he doesn't turn you on. You've never invited him in when he drives you home." Wanda shrugged her shoulders. "I was hoping you were. I am, you know."

"What?" Jenny tried to scoot farther down the mattress.

Wanda noticed and smiled wryly. "Don't worry, Jenny. Your fair white body is in no danger from me. I've got a lover."

Jenny sat in shocked silence while Wanda continued to sip calmly on her Spanada. Jenny heard the rain fall outside, the drip of water from the roof, the hiss of cars on wet pavement. The silence was so complete that she could have heard a clock tick if she had a clock.

"Uuumm." Jenny's voice was strangled.

Wanda sighed. "I'm sorry if I've made you uncomfortable. That wasn't my intent. I just thought that perhaps you were a lesbian, too, and I came over to tell you about a group some of us are forming. I just thought you might like to join."

"Group?"

Wanda saw Jenny's peculiar expression, and sighed. "Not that kind of group. Why is it that straight people invariably attribute a sexual motive to everything a lesbian does? No, woman. It's just a CR group—what the women's movement calls consciousness raising."

Jenny raised her eyebrows. "There are a lot of lesbians in the women's movement?"

Wanda laughed. "If there were, we wouldn't have to be forming this group as an auxiliary. No, almost all of the women are straight and some are a lot like you in that they're scared to death of lesbians. In a way I can see their point, because every time a straight woman

85

gets upset about being treated like a mental retar-
date, some man accuses her of being a lesbian. I guess
that could bother you if you're straight. Sort of like
it really burns me to have someone say that deep down
I'm heterosexual—that my lesbianism is just a mental
hang-up and can be resolved through therapy."

"It's not?" The doubt was plain on Jenny's face.

"No," Wanda said simply. Then a merry look came into her eyes and she added, "Some of my best friends are
men."

Jenny laughed and the atmosphere relaxed.

"Mind if I look at your stuff?" Wanda asked, indicating the paintings.

"I'll give you the guided tour." Jenny got up and
started arranging the canvasses so that Wanda could
see them.

Wanda looked at the canvasses in silence for a few
minutes, paying particular attention to *Breasts.* She
obviously recognized herself. Finally, she breathed
one word, "Wow!"

Surprised (most non-artists were horrified by
Jenny's work), Jenny looked at her.

Wanda stood shaking her head in disbelief. "You
know, when you told me you were an artist, I said to
myself—yeah, sure she is. Ain't no way, baby, that redhead has depth. Guess I was wrong." She paused, then
added with a wicked grin, "Just goes to show, you
can't tell a book by its cover."

Jenny and Wanda both laughed at the Lancism.
Then Jenny, slightly puzzled, asked, "What made you
think I had no depth?"

"Well, you don't exactly present the image of a suffering soul, you know. You act as hard as nails."

"Hmmph. What do you expect me to do—wander up
and down the street like the madwoman of Chaillot,
screaming, 'I hurt, I pain, I suffer?' No thanks, I prefer

to do my suffering in private. That's why I'm an artist."

Wanda let that sink in and nodded in agreement. "I see. Say, can I come to your exhibit? I really, really like your work."

She had said the magic word and Jenny hurriedly took down her address so that she could send her an invitation to the opening. "It's only a few weeks off, now."

The two, friendly and comfortable now, started drinking in earnest, telling jokes, laughing, and sympathizing with one another's problems.

"You might get a lot out of joining the women's movement, you know," Wanda said. "It's nice to know that you're not the Lone Ranger. Besides it'll help you learn to communicate with your fellow women."

"Oh, I like women just fine," Jenny said. "Anyway. I don't have time to join anything."

"Are you sure you like women?" Wanda asked. "You were scared to death of me when I told you I was a lesbian."

Jenny blushed. "Yes—well—that's different."

Wanda grinned. "Afraid you were going to get raped, eh?"

Jenny laughed in embarrassed agreement.

Wanda smiled at her. "Ah. The fear of lesbianism. For years men have told women that there could be no such thing as true friendship between a man and a woman because of the sexual attraction and that Platonic love was impossible because of it. But now, that type of thinking has been transferred to straight women and lesbians. Men say, 'You can't be friends with a lesbian because sooner or later she'll try to get into your pants.' "

Jenny choked and Wanda grinned wickedly. "Not as broadminded as you thought you were, eh?"

"Guess not. Shit. You've just blown my whole number."

"My mission in life." A merry laugh.

"Uh, can I ask you a personal question?" Jenny ventured.

"Let me guess. You want to know what a nice girl like me is doing in a situation like this." Jenny nodded and Wanda smiled. "I really couldn't say. You listen to the shrinks and they say it's because of your childhood—that it was all screwed up, that your parents were playing the wrong roles. But none of that seems to fit me. I'm not saying that isn't the case with some lesbians—like Donna, my lover." Here a look of tenderness crossed her face. "She had a terrible childhood. Her father raped her when she was six—oh, don't look so shocked, Jenny. That happens pretty often, ask any psychiatrist or policeman. Anyway, she had a rough time and is paranoid about men to this day. But me? There aren't many people who had a more normal childhood than I did. My parents weren't crazy, I never got raped, I've slept with men and enjoyed it—but I just happen to prefer women. I've thought about it a lot and I really can't see where my lesbianism could be the result of pathology like the shrinks would have me believe. I even like men, although I sure get sick of having them try to take me to bed when they find out I'm a lesbian. God, nothing seems to turn a man on more than the idea that a woman is a lesbian! They keep thinking that all they have to do to reform us is give us a good fuck." She laughed. "I admire their altruism, but I've had good fucks with men and I still prefer women."

Jenny was fascinated. "Do your parents know?"

"Yes. I told them four years ago—when I came out of the closet."

"How did they take it?"

Wanda sighed. "Well, they didn't exactly jump up and down in celebration. But Dad's accepted it and doesn't bug me about it. It's Mom who has given me the most trouble."

"Come to think of it, it's my mother who has given me the most trouble about my life, too."

Wanda nodded. "I think it has something to do with the way our mothers have lived their lives. They invest a whole lifetime in a certain code of morals—of ethics— and let's face it: a lifetime is a hell of an investment. Then along come their daughters who find nothing valid in their mother's lives, and are determined to live in a completely different way. That's a big shock. And also there's the fact that society has traditionally made mothers the scapegoats for everything that ever goes wrong with their children. And for most people today, lesbianism is still 'going wrong.' "

They were quiet for a moment, reflecting on mothers' sins, children's sins against them. Jenny knew that what Wanda said had validity. How else explain Jenny's mother's constant hysteria over Jenny's life?

"By the way," Wanda broke the silence. "How's your love life, normal one?" A malicious grin.

Jenny blushed. "Well, if you call one-night-stands a love life, it's going great guns."

Shaking her head, Wanda said, "No. I wouldn't. That's a sex life and there's a big difference."

"I know that. But that's all I dare have these days. A real love life is a luxury I can't afford."

"Why?"

"Oh, everytime I get emotionally involved with a man, it turns into nothing but a big rip-off. I can't stand it anymore, getting my hopes up, thinking I've found someone who cares for me, and then finding out that the man I love considers me unacceptable the way I am. Maybe one night stands aren't the greatest, but at least the worst thing I'll get from them is VD—and that's curable."

"Ever try looking at it from the man's viewpoint?"

Wanda asked, pouring herself some more Spanada.

"Humph. Who has to look at it? They're busy all the time screaming it at you. The Sermon on the fucking Mount."

"Well, they have their problems, too, Jenny. After all, they live in the same society that we do and I sometimes think that it's no more fair to them than it is to women. How would you like having to put on a show of invulnerability all the time? Hell, it must drive the poor bastards half crazy. But if a man doesn't do that, then he's called a weakling," and here she smiled bitterly, "or a homosexual."

Jenny was surprised. "That's weird. A lesbian defending men."

Wanda gave a short laugh. "Maybe it's easier for me to see their point of view. I'm not emotionally involved."

As if the atmosphere had gotten too oppressive, Wanda suddenly reached down into her purse. "Let me show you a picture of my girlfriend, Donna." She took out her wallet, opened it, and thrust it at Jenny: "Here. We had that taken last year at Disneyland."

Jenny looked down. There was a remarkably ugly young woman seated in a wheelchair in front of the Magic Palace. Wanda was standing beside her, a hand on the woman's shoulder. Both were smiling into the camera.

Wanda's voice was husky. "She's the most beautiful person in the world."

Hours later, having killed the bottle of Spanada, Wanda rose tipsily to go. Jenny staggered with her to the door and took her hand. "Peace, sister," she said.

Wanda smiled. "Thank you." She squeezed Jenny's hand and left, wading down the street through the falling rain.

Spring was a long time coming. One day the rain would increase; the next day the clouds would briefly part, bringing hopeful Angelenos rushing out of their stucco apartments; then just as quickly the clouds would close again, drenching them in liquid sunshine. Jenny had given up waiting for the sun. She carried a new umbrella (trophy of her improved financial position) everywhere and more often than not, used it. She had new waterproof boots covering her sneakers and on Fridays, Saturdays, and Sundays, they covered her platform shoes.

She had adjusted more quickly than she had thought possible to her schizophrenic role in life—by day, dedicated artist; by night Koy Kitten. It seemed to be leaving no obvious scars on her soul. The painting which had evolved out of this peculiar existence, *Breasts*, showed signs of becoming Jenny's best work. Unlike her other paintings it was gaudy and raw but immensely powerful. She worked on it with a growing sense of awe.

As the weeks went by, Jenny's arm grew stronger and her shoulders ceased to ache from the weight of the frosted beer mugs. She developed a rapport with the dancers, Wanda and Janine, with Lance, and even with the customers. And they, in turn, learned to adjust to Jenny.

"You can catch more flies with honey than you can with vinegar," Lance would admonish when he overheard Jenny snarling at a customer.

"Turn thou the other cheek," Wanda would crack from the platform as a drunken customer pinched Jenny's rear.

Lance taught Jenny how to recognize a potential

problem customer. "You can hear them breathe," he explained. "And don't make the mistake of blaming it on the smog. Just be cool and remember—where there's smoke, there's fire."

Completely unmanageable customers, fortunately, were a rarity. Most would slump in squelched silence at a stern reprimand—the few who didn't were escorted out the door by a platitude-spouting Lance; they rarely returned.

The days began to blur together and Jenny only became conscious of the passage of time when she entered the Pink Pussy to find everyone wearing green.

"Sure and begorra, it's the little lass," chirped Lance, dancing toward her with a green bowler on his head and a shamrock pinned to his green striped shirt.

The Pink Pussy, for tonight only, had become the Green Pussy. Green crepe paper hung from the ceiling in ribboned curlicues, huge metallic green shamrocks were pasted to the pink walls. The air was electric with the vibrations of clashing colors.

"Shit," Jenny muttered, dodging away from the shamrock Lance was trying to pin in her hair.

"Mouth," Lance reminded her. "Remember, the Pink Pussy likes its barmaids to be ladies." He grabbed a hank of her hair and fastened the shamrock to her. "There now . . . a real Irish colleen."

Jenny twisted her mouth into a sneer; when it came to celebrations and holidays, she was an Ebenezer Scrooge. Ticky-tacky, she thought. Still, she arranged the shamrock more securely and walked past a green-clad, grinning Mo to the dressing room.

Janine was there; she was dancing early that day, Wanda taking the later shift. She looked up at Jenny and gave a vague, woozy "Hi."

Tranquilizers again, Jenny thought. Janine was a tall brunette beauty but the blank look on her face was not an entirely natural expression. Janine, to put it bluntly, was always legally stoned. "Nerves," she would explain as she popped another pill. "I've got bad nerves. The doctor says so."

Janine adjusted her green vinyl boots (a shamrock pasted to the side of each) and gave some finishing pats to her hair. "Well, I'm off."

"You sure are," Jenny said sadly under her breath as the dancer groggily departed. When Jenny got out on the floor minutes later, Janine was dancing animatedly to "Mother's Little Helper."

"How's my favorite Colleen?" Mo asked as she served him a beer.

"Still trying, eh?" Jenny smiled at him. Mo was coming in every night she was on now, sitting at the same table grinning the same wolfish grin. He would sit for hours, writing on his current book when she was busy with other customers. "Hemingway wrote in bars," he explained. "So I guess I can write *The Princess and the Beanpole* in one."

"Kiddie book?"

"No, Mama," he grinned.

Jenny laughed and walked away shaking her head.

The night went by swiftly. Customers would come in rain-soaked, water dripping off green bowlers and shamrocks, sit hunched over their frosted mugs for an hour, and then depart. Few stayed for long. The big action that night was at the Irish bar down the street where word had it that several grand fights were going on. When the door was open, the blows could actually be heard along with loud shouts and laughter.

"The national pasttime," Mo cracked as a particularly loud crash reverberated down the street.

"Keeps them out of trouble," Jenny answered with a yawn.

"Tired?"

"Yeah. I got up early this morning to work. I've almost finished *Breasts*. God, the damn thing's so big it's taken me a month of steady work."

Mo looked suitably impressed. "When can I see it?"

"You can come to the opening. It's only two weeks away."

"Oh." He looked disappointed, but didn't press the point. Persistency, he had learned, was the secret of success.

Lance closed the bar early and Jenny hopped in the Porsche gratefully. Once in the studio, she fell, exhausted, into bed—the shamrock still twisted into her long, red hair.

The next day Jenny had reserved for Freebies. Freebies were drawings, signs, and the various odds and ends which artists' friends thought the artist would be only too glad to do for them. "After all, it isn't really work, is it?" they would say as they made their request. And Jenny, grinding her teeth in silence, would say, "Yeah, sure. Be glad to do it for you."

On her list: One: a pastel portrait of Mo's father for Mo's mother and a cover design for one of his books. Two: a sign for Lance telling the world at large that you had to be twenty-one to enter the Pink Pussy. Three: a pastel portrait of Wanda for Wanda's girlfriend. Four: a pastel portrait of Janine for Janine. Five: a water color for Angela from Sushi ("You're so much better at that sort of thing than I am, Jen. Besides, she already has six of my paintings and God knows how many sketches. This will give her a little diversification.") Six: a pen and ink sketch of Silver for Lou.

This last had never been requested. Lou was the only one of her friends who never asked for bits and pieces of art work. But she hadn't seen Lou since the day she had insulted Silver and she knew this would help pave

the way to a reconciliation. Jenny sometimes treated
her friends cavalierly, but she nonetheless valued them.
For Lou, she would draw Silver's dewlap chops.

She worked all day. The air was choked with the dust
from the pastel crayons; she wheezed and her eyes ran.
This was a warning of what the summer would be like.
Every summer she wandered into one of the many
Southern California tourist traps, armed with her pas-
tels and an easel, and proceeded to draw children,
dogs, cats, and pants-suited matrons. But as she worked,
she forced her mind away from this vision of her future.
As Lance would no doubt say, she'd cross that bridge
when she came to it.

She worked quickly, wanting to deliver the sketches
before work that evening. *Breasts* stared balefully down
at her from its easel. Finally, around four, she was finished, and resolutely, she tucked the work under her
arm and marched off through the rain to Lou's.

She knocked nervously at Lou's door. A suspicious
eye peered out. "Aha. Greeks bearing gifts, I see. Oh
well. Come on in."

More relieved than she cared to admit, Jenny walked
in. The tv was going. No Silver was present. "Uh, Lou.
I thought you might like to have these." She hated to
let Lou see how embarrassed she was. "I mean—I know
I've been a little too much lately, but you know . . ."

"You know how it is," Lou finished for her.

"Yeah," Jenny smiled. "You know how it is."

Lou accepted the portrait with real joy, propping it
up on the color tv. Then she turned to an additional
piece Jenny had brought—a self-portrait.

"Beautiful, Jen. Just beautiful. But you know, you're
the only woman I've ever met who doesn't flatter herself. Just look at the face in that portrait. You've made
yourself look like a hag."

It was true. Jenny had painted in lines that weren't

there and folds that wouldn't appear for another twenty years—if then. The face that stared out of the painting was an old, tortured face. But it was still Jenny West.

"Why do you do that?" Lou asked.

Jenny knew she would never be able to explain. Beauty, as most people saw it, didn't interest artists. Jenny knew that she had a beautiful face—but why was it considered beautiful? It was smooth, the features were flawless, it was also completely devoid of any hint of character or distinction.

She had observed that when a woman began to develop personality or character in her face other people began to say that she had lost her beauty. Was that what beauty was considered to be, then, in a woman? No visible sign of maturity?

Jenny said, "I just like lines, I guess."

Lou smiled and shook her head. "I don't think I'll ever understand you, Jenny."

"Don't worry about it. I don't understand myself."

They both laughed and their friendship was on again. Jenny settled herself in a chair and, with a glass of wine in her hand, watched the unrequited loves and nervous breakdowns soapsudsed across the screen. During the commercials they chatted.

Lou talked about Silver. "Poor thing. Roxanne's driving him crazy. She's in primal therapy now and is always screaming in the cabana. His nerves are shot. He's seeing me twice a week now."

Jenny was determined to be generous. "Gee. That's nice, Lou."

Lou smiled thinly. "Don't strain yourself."

Jenny blushed.

"I know you don't approve of Silver supporting me, but I don't see things the way you do. Silver wouldn't be faithful to Roxanne anyway—few men are faithful to their wives—and at least, by having me, he does all his messing around in one place. She knows where to reach him in case of emergencies. And as far as her feelings go—well, she has her guitar player and I have Silver."

Jenny grunted, seeing a sort of poetic justice. But then she said, "There's one difference, though. Silver's married to her."

"So?" Lou looked amused. "I don't want to marry Silver."

Jenny was genuinely surprised. "I thought you loved him!"

"I do, I do. But as for being his wife . . . no way. Men are always nicer to their mistresses."

Jenny blinked. "I wouldn't know."

"As it is now, Roxanne is someone he frequently resents. He loves her, in his way, but still she's a legal encumbrance. He can shed me any time he wants. But I can do the same. He knows it and I know it. So we're voluntary. I wouldn't change that for the world."

Jenny sat in surprised silence.

Lou continued, "I was a little girl once, too. You weren't the only one. When I remember my parents I cringe. Happily married they were. I saw enough of that to last me for a lifetime. What they did to each other every day would be forbidden under the terms of the Geneva Convention. But since they were married it was considered okay. A license to kill, marriage is. Not right away, perhaps, but a little every day until you've finished the other person off. God, I'll never get married!"

"But what about when you get old?"

"Oh, I'll be all right. Silver is more generous than you think. I have a nice, fat savings account and a pretty decent stock portfolio. I've done as much as I can with what I've got—which (you'll have to admit) isn't much. I'm not talented. I'll never be even pretty, I can't type,

97

I don't have a degree. The only thing I can do is hold a man. So that's what I do."

Jenny stared at the television screen where an elegantly gowned beauty was waxing a floor. She looked back up at Lou and held out her hand. "Truce."

Lou took it and smiled. "Different strokes, Jen."

"I guess we agree on something, then," said Jenny. "Like about marriage. But you still believe in love, right?"

"Right," said Lou. "But voluntary."

"I don't know," Jenny mused. "I think maybe you say that because you don't have anything else that you consider valuable. Something that could be taken from you."

"I don't see what you mean."

Jenny said, "Well, it seems to me that love is a luxury. A nice pasttime for the secure and unthreatened. Death of the body isn't the only thing to be afraid of, Lou. There are other kinds of death. Worse ones."

"Like you with Ken?" Lou was beginning to understand.

Jenny nodded sadly. "Yes. He killed a little bit of me each day—just like you were saying about your parents. He did it with kindness—and with love—but the result was just the same."

"But he offered you security, too. You would have been able to paint without worrying about where your next meal was coming from."

Jenny grimaced. "Yeah, sure. Except for one thing. An artist can't create without spiritual freedom and unfortunately security and freedom can't live under the same roof."

"I find that hard to believe. Look at all the artists who were married. Even Picasso!"

Jenny smiled at that. "They were men. Nobody expects them to drop everything and fix dinner."

98

They sat in silence for a while, listening to the griefs of the tube. One thing about soaps, Jenny thought, they dulled the mind. And maybe that wasn't always such a bad thing.

During another commercial Lou said, "Get the brochures for the exhibit printed yet?"

"No. Pearce is doing that. I saw him about it the other day."

"Just one more to go," she had told him. He had looked alarmed, his thin face becoming more pinched than usual. "Will it be ready?"

It was an acrylic, she had assured him. Dry almost upon completion.

"I hear you've been having some bad luck lately," he had probed gently.

"Oh. Nothing catastrophic. Just had to get a job, that's all."

"Too bad," he had said, folding his dry, wrinkled hands. "Where? Doing what?"

Sighing, Jenny had told him all about the Pink Pussy, adding, "Listen, I'd rather you not let it get around. It could hurt my professional reputation; the idea that I can't support myself with my painting."

Pearce had nodded his head. "You have my solemn word, my dear. It shall never pass my lips." His eyelids slid slowly over small, dark eyes.

Lou was asking, "Your opening's just two weeks away, isn't it?"

"Yeah. Two weeks." Jenny's hand shook a little.

"Wow."

"Yeah. Wow."

There was another silence, then Lou said, "Don't worry, Jen. I have this feeling about it. I think this might just be the big one."

Jenny couldn't help but smile. Lou had said the same thing about her previous exhibits but then friends always saw genius in each other. That's what they were for.

"I sure hope you're right, Lou. I'm getting pretty sick of roughing it."

The next morning Jenny read the flyer that had arrived in the mail.

OILS AND ACRYLICS
by
JENNIFER LOUISE WEST

* * * * * * * * * * * * ** * * * * * * * * * * * * *

Jennifer West is a Bar Maid.
Jennifer West is an Artist.
Can the two beings inhabit the same lovely body?
The Pearce Gallery is very pleased, very proud to
announce quite firmly that they can. Oh, yes.
They most certainly can. Come and see this
exciting, beautiful exhibit by this
exciting, beautiful woman.

Refreshments served. BankAmericard.

"That prick," Jenny hissed.

The next day started ominously. In the morning the toilet overflowed, sending a soggy, disgusted Jenny on a trip through the rain to a pay phone. "Pee in a can!" Carlos shrieked. "Why bother me with your bowel habits? Everybody knows you artists are nothing but

100

peegs, anyway!"

Jenny pleaded and Carlos finally agreed to send a
repairman over the next day. If he could get one. "In
the meantime, don't drink water. Eat coconut." He
slammed down the phone.

Then, fixing lunch, she opened a can of chili and
watched as the top slid back into the can. She stuck a
finger down to drag it out and gashed herself on the
ragged edge, bleeding profusely into the beans. "Oh
well," she thought. "More protein." Visions of the
Donner party loped through her mind.

And so it went for the rest of the day. As she was
working on *Breasts* a brush snapped. It was old and dry
rot had finished off the wood. Unfortunately, it was a
fine, small detail brush and would have to be replaced
right away. At least she had the money. She could make
the trip to Howard's and go directly from there to the
Pink Pussy.

There was little rain that day, which should have
been a good omen, but Jenny felt strangely apprehen-
sive. Rain and misery seemed to be her lot in life—why
should it stop now? The gods didn't forget their enemy
list that easily.

Gingerly, she stepped out of the studio.

All quiet on the western front. No bombs dropped,
the San Andreas fault didn't open up—all seemed normal (for Southern California). At the top of Normandie
Hill was even a sure sign of spring—a skateboarding
sidewalk surfer. Relaxing, she set off down Beverly
Boulevard.

She heard the whine of the skateboard behind her—
it was gaining, picking up speed as it neared the bottom
of the hill. The surfer was going too fast for safety.
Jenny stepped into a doorway and out of his path. She
was taking no chances.

The surfer was almost at the bottom of the hill.

He was ready for the turn onto Beverly. His raincoat flapped in the breeze.

With a scream of wheels, he whipped around the corner and onto the level Boulevard. He slowed as he approached Jenny's doorway.

He was no teenager. He was fifty if he was a day. And he looked familiar. His raincoat was open. So were his pants.

He swept by her with a triumphant leer, his upright penis leading the way.

When she finally reached the bar after stopping by Howard's she found the Pink Pussy in turmoil. Lance almost fell over Jenny as she came through the door. "Grandma's back! She's coming in! To inspect!" He paused for breath. "Now don't get me wrong—I've missed her. Absence makes the heart grow fonder. But we've got to get this place cleaned up. Wipe the tables! Empty the ashtrays! Throw out the perverts!"

The place buzzed with action. The dancers were putting Erase on appendix scars, applying blusher to their nipples, putting gems in navels. All getting shipshape for Gramdma.

At nine o'clock that evening Elzie Wyzenski rolled in.

She was not your basic little old lady. Painted like a canvas, wrinkled like a raisin, she nonetheless sat on her wheelchair like a throne. Jenny could hardly repress a cheer of "Long live the Queen!" The old lady's thin legs were encased in white vinyl boots which reached almost up to the thigh length white knit dress. Perched on the flaming red hair was a baby blue jockey cap. Elzie Wyzenski was not ageing gracefully. Jenny surmised that she had decided to fight old age to the death.

Lance hovered near, mouthing inanities, but the old lady waved him away with green tipped fingers. "Don't bug me, Caroll."

Caroll? Jenny grinned and Lance blushed and fled behind the bar.

"Stupid boy, that," Mrs. Wyzenski said. She barked like a seal. "You. Red. You an actress?"

Jenny smiled. "No. I'm a painter."

Mrs. Wyzenski barked again. It was a laugh. "You have my sympathies. Any artist living in Culture Gulch does." She looked at the ceiling. "Me—I took the easy way out. I was a beauty when I was young and I milked it for all it was worth. It's the only smart thing to do. If you're a woman. You get too much shit trying it the other way." She shook her head. "Well, let's see what's been going on since I've been gone."

She rolled around the bar, inspecting everything carefully. She paid particular attention to the dancers' dressing room—looking at the floor to see if it was clean, checking the dressing table for pills. She turned up the thermostat, muttering "Let those bastard politicians walk around topless in a sixty-five degree room and they'd stop talking about sacrifice pretty quick. My dancers aren't going to freeze for them or anybody else." She motioned Jenny over to her. "Tell me about your painting. You just talk about it or have you exhibited?"

Sensing a kindred spirit, Jenny answered, "I've had two shows and a third is coming up this month."

"So you got this job until your exhibit. Then you'll quit."

Jenny blushed and Mrs Wyzenski grinned. "Don't worry about it. This is L.A. Beautiful girls are a dime a dozen. But consider yourself at home."

"Thank you." Jenny had felt a strong and immediate liking for this tough old woman. "Your grandson is nice to work for."

Mrs. Wyzenski barked, "Caroll? He's an ass. Can't see any farther than his mirror."

At closing time Lance loaded the wheel chair in his Porsche and left Jenny to face the two blocks to her studio alone. She wasn't too worried. Beverly Boulevard was a well-lit street with plenty of traffic. She would be all right.

But now, the same street which looked so tame and mediocre during daylight was sinister with shadows. The streetlamps seemed farther apart, their light dimmer. Clutching her package from Howard's to her breast, Jenny walked nervously down the street staying as close as possible to the curb. No sense in taking chances.

She remembered part of her conversation with Mrs. Wyzenski. The old lady had confided to Jenny that in her youth she had frequently wished that she had been born a man. "So they would leave me alone, you see." It had crossed Jenny's mind, too. Being a man had its good points. For instance, a man wouldn't have so much to fear walking down Beverly Boulevard at two in the morning. And a man could hitchhike across the country with pretty good chances of making it unmolested. Jenny had never been able to make it farther than the end of the block.

She wondered—if she could, would she lay down those ladies' chains? Would she rather be a man?

She started to make a list of the advantages of being a man.

One: you could pick anybody up and not be called a tramp.

Two: you'd know how to fix stereos, light switches, and toilets.

Three: and speaking of toilets, you'd no longer have to pay a dime to pee.

Four: you could run faster.

Five: you wouldn't have to worry about getting

pregnant.

Six: people would think twice about insulting
you (instead of crying, you would hit them).

Seven: you could get a big dog and live in a house by
yourself in Laurel Canyon and be considered a rugged
individualist instead of a weird broad.

Eight: you could open stuck doors.

At that point, Jenny decided to drop the whole
thing. It was getting too depressing.

She was only one block from her studio now, and she
began to relax. Home free.

Then.

Like they say in the comics. Zap!

Jenny was having trouble breathing because a huge,
hairy hand was wrapped around her throat. And something sharp was pressed against her back.

Oh Lord God. This was IT.

Jenny struggled, twisting and turning, trying to get
his hand off her throat, trying to get around to face him.
Fat lot of good that police whistle ever-present around
her neck was doing here. She barely could breathe, let
alone grab and blow the damn thing. If she came
through this alive she was going to visit that cop on
tv who had suggested all women carry one. She'd
shove it—chain and all— right up his broadbeamed ass.

If she didn't get some air she was going to pass out.
Oh, please! Just be a rapist, not a murderer. Jenny
hoped he realized that she wanted to finish her painting. She wanted to see Paris. The great pyramid. She
wanted to get to do everything she wouldn't be able
to do if he killed her.

He was trying to drag her around the corner and out
of the vision of the occasional passing car. Jenny knew
that street. Bushes galore. Dark. Dark as sin.

He loosed his grip on her throat in order to grab her
hands which were clawing wildly at him. She could

breathe again.

He hissed the immortal words, "Scream and you're dead."

But, as Jenny's teachers had so frequently complained to her mother, Jenny just wouldn't follow orders.

So she screamed. She sucked in a big, beautiful blast of air and screamed. A full-throated, high-octave, rip-roaring screech. Not just one. A full chorus of yells, bellows and howls. Let the bastard send her to her grave—she'd take his eardrums with her.

Her assailant spun her around to face him. "Holy shit, woman. Shut up! I just wanna get me a little."

Prince Charming he wasn't. Even in Jenny's petrified state she had to admit that he presented a good case for rape. He was a cross between Lon Chaney's Phantom of the Opera and a blind date. He had an ugly scarred-up face (the scars left there by his previous victims, no doubt) and green teeth. His mamma had never told him about Ultra-Brite.

Not letting compassion get the best of her, Jenny screamed and flailed on. For Christ sake, wasn't any-body going to help her? This wasn't New York.

Somebody!

Help!

Then, in between screams, she heard a window slide open. Thank God. But then a male voice called out, "For Christ's sake, can't a person get some sleep around here?"

"Help! Help!" Jenny screamed. "Rape!"

The voice said, "Everybody knows a woman can't be raped if she doesn't want to be." And the window slammed down.

"Help! Help!" Jenny was crying now: her assail-ant was giggling.

"See, sweetheart? Ain't nobody gonna help you. Now be a good girl and hold still."

He wrestled her to the pavement. God. This was really it. Lying on her back beneath him, she was surprised to find that she still had her brush from Howard's.

"Hey, sweetheart. How'd ya like it best? Front or back?"

Well, at least he asked.

He had his hand on her throat again and she could no longer scream. Not that it had worked wonders, anyway. He was ripping her sweater.

She closed her eyes. She sure as hell wasn't going to watch.

"Hubba, hubba," he was saying.

Maybe it would be quick. Maybe he was a premature ejaculator.

But wait! The ghost of the beloved Pablo nudged her. She had a weapon!

She tightened her fingers around the long, thin handle of the Grumbacher Red Sable number two. And started stabbing.

The screaming began again but this time in a full, rich baritone. On and on she hacked, the brush became an ice pick.

Blood poured.

Her attacker rolled off, his hands shielding his face; "Help!" he screamed. "Help, help!"

Tires squealed to a halt, windows and doors flew open, everywhere was heard in the land the sound of running feet.

Saved!

Jenny lay exhausted on the pavement, trying feebly to hold the ripped fragments of her sweater together. Modesty at all times. The man lay next to her, sobbing loudly.

She heard a siren and saw the flashing red light of the patrol car as it rolled toward her. "To serve and protect" was painted on the door. God bless the L.A.P.D.

"What's going on here?" a uniformed man asked;

"She tried to kill me, officer," Jenny's attacker sobbed. "I'm blinded for life."

The next thing Jenny knew, she was being hauled to her feet and handcuffed.

"Hey. Wait a minute. That guy attacked me. Arrest him. Look at my clothes. Doesn't that tell you something?" Her ripped sweater had fallen open and there was Jenny underneath.

Badge 8941 said, "Sure. Looks like the poor guy was trying to defend himself." He was fresh-faced, shiny-clean.

The older officer, Badge 3742, was a plump, unclean man. "No one heard a woman scream," he pointed out.

They both looked at her accusingly, their faces filled with the cynicism that only the uniformed can manage.

An ambulance arrived for the sobbing man. He was solicitously trundled into it and driven off to the loving care of Central Receiving. Jenny was dragged to the patrol car.

"Officer. Honest. I was just trying to defend myself," she protested. "He told me to be quiet or he'd kill me."

Badge 3742 said, "I say that to my wife twice a day. That doesn't give her the right to launch a vicious attack."

Badge 8941 looked at him and beamed. "Hey. Great phrase. Vicious attack." He wrote it down. "I'm writing a book," he explained to Jenny. "About you perverts."

"And by the way," Badge 3742 said. "Do you have a license for carrying around a concealed weapon?"

"Weapon?" Jenny was starting to get hysterical all over again. "That's a Grumbacher number two. I'm an artist."

The two policemen looked at each other. "An artist!" they chorused. Their faces became grim. 3742 said to

108

8941, "My nephew Francis is one of them artists. Voted for McGovern."

They turned back to her. "Look. We got your number, freak. You might as well come along quietly."

Jenny started to cry.

8941 smiled happily. "Look," he said, writing in his little notebook. "Tears of remorse!"

Salvation finally came over the patrol car radio, relaying the information that one Murray J. Gaston, alias Joseph Barrett, alias Seymour Feldman, was wanted for the rape of eleven women, one seventy-five years old, one nine.

"I guess we'll have to let her go," 3742 sighed.

"We can hold her for disturbing the peace," Badge 8941 said hopefully.

"Better not. Still, it's a shame. Damn women are always asking for it."

Jenny started to yell, "Wait a minute! I was coming home, minding my own business. I was not asking for it!"

8941 sneered. "All women secretly want to be raped. I read it in the L. A. Times. A psychologist said it and he ought to know more about it than you."

"Oh yeah?" Jenny sneered. "Well, Freud said that every man has a death wish, too. So why don't you give me a medal for helping that bastard along with his?"

"What a foul mouth," 3742 said. "Goddamn broads. Always making trouble." They pushed her out of the patrol car.

Standing there, clutching her torn clothes, Jenny asked, "Aren't you going to take me home?"

Badge 8941 spat as they drove away. "Look, lady. This isn't a taxi service."

Jenny woke up crying the next morning. Shaking, remembering that it was not a dream, she got out of bed and walked sniffling to the easel. Without even heating up a cup of coffee she began to work, holding the brush steady with two hands.

"Shit," she whimpered, as her shaking hand pushed the brush into areas she had not meant it to go. "Oh shit," she mourned.

As the morning wore on, the paint began to flow freely and, conversely, her tears dried up. Last night's experience was forgotten. By the time she was ready for work at the Pink Pussy that evening, she had returned to normal. Or what passed for normal with Jenny West.

It wasn't raining, just overcast, but Jenny took her umbrella along with her anyway. It had a sharp, steel point on the end and she grimly thought that it might come in handy. More hesitantly than usual, she began the walk through the gloom to the Pink Pussy. The blinking pink lights had come into view when a hand grabbed her arm.

Jenny swung the umbrella around with a yell. She would fight to the death, she had decided.

"Hey, hey, Jennifer. Lighten up."

Jenny dropped the umbrella and looked up to see the face of the only man she had ever loved.

"Hello, Ken." Her voice surprised her, it was so steady.

Ken smiled down at her, the ghost of Christmas past. "It's been a long four years." He hadn't changed. His sideburns were a little fuller, his moustache drooped lower, but he was still the same handsome, rakish Ken.

Jenny took a few deep breaths before she said, "Well. You're looking fine. How have you been?" Slow. Casual. Steady.

110

"I've been fine. I saw a friend of yours a little while back. She wouldn't give me your address."

Jenny smiled. Good old Lou. Aloud, she said, "Well, she knows how I feel."

Ken raised his eyebrows. "You haven't changed? You've had some years to think it over, years to live that artist's life you wanted so much. And as someone who really cares, I'll have to say that you don't look like it's been a resounding success."

Jenny blushed, aware of her patched denims, her torn T-shirt and dirty sneakers. "I don't dress for others," she proclaimed haughtily. "What do you expect me to paint in—a bustle?"

"Still the same old bitch, I see." Ken drew his mouth into a thin, disapproving line.

Jenny looked at him in silence, remembering the day four years ago when he had last called her a bitch. It had been their wedding day.

She had been in her studio, painting, concentrating on a particularly difficult problem in the upper right corner of the canvas, whistling as she worked. She was painting, happy, secure in herself and her existence.

There had come a knocking and banging at the door— a deep male voice screaming invectives. Jenny dropped her brush in alarm, then gasped in horror as Ken broke down the door.

"Forget something?" he inquired, a black look on his face.

"Oh my God," Jenny gasped. "Oh God—oh, holy shit!" She sank to the floor and sat there, shaking, her hands covering her face. She shook her head back and forth in anguish. It was two o'clock. At noon she was supposed to have been at church. With Ken. Getting married. And she had forgotten.

Feeling her heart try to burst out of its confining space, Jenny dropped her hands and looked up at Ken.

Because of temporary insanity, perhaps, she tried to be funny. "Well, hon. Love means never having to say you're sorry."

Then it came. "Bitch!" he screamed at her. "You rotten, shitty, flippant bitch!"

Jenny, in alarm, got shakily to her feet. Ken seemed to be going wild with rage and she wanted to be able to get out of his way, out of the studio and into the protection of the open street—where passers-by might stop a man from killing a woman. "K-Ken," she stuttered. "I'm . . . I'm . . . oh, shit. I'm *sorry*."

"Sorry?" Ken screamed. "You stand me up at the church and you have the nerve to stand there and tell me you're *sorry*?"

"Oh, Ken. I forgot. Please. I just forgot."

"Like hell you did! Freud said there are no such things as accidents and he was right. How do you think I felt waiting there with all those hairy, vermin-infested freaks you call your friends? I'll never forgive you. You've embarrassed me in front of my business associates!"

Jenny was still shaking but she was finding her voice. "Freud be damned, Ken. I didn't do this on purpose. I forgot."

"Freud's never wrong!" he yelled back.

The door was hanging on one hinge and their screaming voices had collected the usual crowd of excitement seekers. A growing number of men, women, and children were collecting outside, peering into the studio in interest. In the true, ever-partisan spirit of the mob, they were choosing up sides. Ken was the heavy favorite. "He's right," a thin male voice piped. "Old Daddy Freud was a right-on cat. Especially where women were concerned." There was the sound of a spit.

Ken rushed around the studio in near-demented rage. The crowd had given him the support he needed and he, with great self-righteousness, began knocking canvasses over. "They mean more to you than I do!" he cried, watching them fall over. "Rags and chemicals. Nothing. They're nothing! And yet you prefer them to me. You're a sick, unnatural bitch!"

Jenny watched in horror as he grabbed up a palette knife and slashed at a giant oil drying against the door. "There! You see how durable they are. Love lasts forever and you're throwing in with these canvas rags." Having slashed that canvas to shreds, he turned to her paint-box, dumped it onto the floor and started grinding tubes under his wing-tipped shoes. Bright streams of color ejaculated onto the wall. Reds, yellows, blues, all the colors she was painting in those days. All the bright, happy colors.

The crowd cheered as Ken left the tubes of paint, grabbed the palette knife again, and started toward another large canvas. He was bent on the destruction of Jenny's studio.

"No!" Jenny cried. "No!" Her fear and horror changed to anger as she saw she was about to lose the results of several months of agonizing, exhausting work. "Leave them alone!"

Ken turned to face her and laughed demonically. "Aha! See? I was right! They're all you care about." Still laughing, he slashed at an acrylic.

Slowly, calmly, Jenny picked up another palette knife—a large straight one she used for mixing clotted pigments. She heard her voice coming as if from far away. "Get your prick out of here before I carve a bas-relief on it!"

Jenny meant it, and Ken, seeing her white, determined face, began to edge slowly to the door. "You're going to regret this!"

"Probably," Jenny whispered. "But get out just the same. And don't come back."

There was total silence in the studio—the crowd hushed its buzz. Everyone was waiting to see what Ken would do. Would he take her in his arms, forgive all in a tearful, impassioned scene just like in the movies?

"Fucking cunt," Ken hissed, threw down the palette knife, and left.

This was life—real life, decided the crowd. They parted in respectful silence as Ken strode to the curb where his Mercedes was parked and applauded politely when he turned and gave Jenny the finger.

"What a man!" one of the women breathed in admiration as he drove off.

Jenny stood in the middle of the studio, alone, shaking. Several paintings had been ruined—several months of work to be done all over. She looked down at her hand, still clutching the palette knife. It's shaking, she thought. That's funny. I don't feel a thing. Why should my hand shake? Her legs, suddenly tired, suddenly weak, slumped, and Jenny sank to a sitting position on the floor, staring numbly at the wall where bright rivers of color crossed each other. An interesting pattern, she thought. Might be able to do something with that.

The crowd was still milling around and Jenny was still sitting on the floor when her parents arrived. They had flown in from Detroit for the wedding. Her mother, mink-caped and orchid-corsaged, stared at the studio in distaste. "Fine mess you've made, Little Miss Artist. I wouldn't be so snotty if I were you; you can't even paint a decent still life. You'd be better off learning how to cook!"

Jenny picked herself up off the floor and rubbed her eyes wearily. "Mother—please try to understand. I'm not so bad."

Her mother sneered. "No man will ever respect you unless you change your ways. You're selfish!"

Jenny looked around at the remainder of her work

and answered bitterly, "It takes a certain amount of courage for a woman to be selfish these days." She turned her back to her mother and began wiping the paint off the walls.

"Courage? Ha! The only kind of courage a man wants in his woman is the courage it takes to sacrifice herself for him. What good is all this doing you?"

"It makes me happy," Jenny answered simply, looking at the rag in her hand. The red paint on it looked like bloodstains.

"Since when is a woman supposed to be happy?" her mother screamed. "You think I've been happy with your father? Being happy is none of a woman's business. She's supposed to make other people happy!"

She wrapped her mink more tightly around her and sailed out the door and into the sympathetic crowd, leaving Jenny's father, forgotten, standing quietly in the corner.

Looking sadly at his wife's departing figure, he cleared his throat and said, "Jen—maybe I shouldn't comment. I mean—your mother's just upset." He paused, then continued more firmly, "I was always a meat and potatoes man, but your mother told me when we first got married that she wanted to really put herself out for me—make things that were really complicated, you know? So I wound up with twenty-eight years of tuna noodle casseroles."

He smiled bleakly and left.

So it was a small world, just like everybody said. They stood there, on the same corner, four years later. Jenny—an older Jenny—smiled at Ken. "Still a flaming liberal? Or did I turn your coat for good?"

"You know me, Jennifer. I think we should impeach the entire GOP and hussle ass out of NATO."

"Should we get out of the UN, too?"

Ken chuckled. "Still politically naive as always, eh, Jennifer? It's the conservative reactionaries who want out of the UN; we liberals just want out of everything else."

"Thanks for making it perfectly clear."

They looked at each other for a moment, then Ken said, "Say, why don't we have dinner together, for old times sake?"

Jenny stiffened. "I thought liberals were against clinging to the past. Oh, sorry. I forgot that nostalgia is in this year."

His face turned cold. "Right. I was just being polite. Something that wouldn't hurt you, now and then. See you around."

"Yeah. We'll have lunch."

With a look that amounted to twenty megatons of overkill, Ken turned and walked off.

Jenny wondered how long it would take for the tears to run down her cheeks to her jaw.

A woman was supposed to give everything to her man but the man could reserve, hold back, keep a part of himself private. That's the way love was supposed to work here in America and here in the twentieth century. There was expected to be no room in a woman's heart for other matters once she had filled it with love. Who the hell developed that philosophy? Jenny knew that it had to have been a man.

To Ken, Jenny's painting had been a mere pasttime, a hobby, something he expected her to spend less time with once they were married. Jenny remembered him saying, "Jennifer, darling, we'll be so busy doing things together. I'll read you my briefs, you can watch me in court when I've got a Civil Rights case—and then, someday, there'll be children. We'll have a full life and there'll be so much to do."

Jenny remembered the old days—the days of warmth.

When Ken talked, Jenny would nestle against him and close her eyes. He sounded so wise, so experienced. Maybe he was right. Maybe she put too much emphasis on all the wrong things.

Like the importance of her studio.

"Jennifer darling. I've found this wonderful house in Encino. The couple has to sell it for the divorce settlement. Let's go out and see it this weekend."

"But Ken. That's too far from my studio."

Ken hugged her. "Sweetheart. You won't be needing that smelly studio. This house has a nice large kitchen. I thought of you the minute I saw it. You'll be able to paint and cook at the same time."

The house was beautiful, all right. It was in perfect taste. Four bedrooms. ("One will be my den and there will still be two left for the children.") A large dining room. ("We'll do a lot of entertaining; you'll have to learn to cook gourmet dishes—something really esoteric, like Indian food.") The living room had a step-down conversation pit in front of the fireplace. ("I can just see us sitting here after supper—you'll be doing needlepoint as I work on my briefs.") But the piece de resistance was the neighbors.

"Oh, Jennifer, wait until you meet the woman in the pink house. You'll just love her. She used to be an art teacher before she got married; now she belongs to the Ladies' Guild and she promised to get you in. And the other one . . . guess?"

Jenny couldn't guess.

"She paints!" Ken sang happily. "The cutest pictures of children. Just like those Keane paintings. Big eyes. She says you can join the Encino Art Club. She's the president. They have teas once a month."

Jenny had clung tightly to him. "Oh, Ken. I love you so much!"

117

"Why, Jennifer. You're shaking. You sweet little thing."

He had kissed her right there in front of the smiling neighbors.

Looking back, clear-eyed, over the years, Jenny saw that, indeed, Freud had been right on one score. There were damn few accidents. You didn't forget your wedding day without a reason.

She sighed and waved hello to Lance and Mrs. Wyzenski. She would be all right. It hurt a little less each year.

The weather didn't seem to be changing as April peered soggily around the corner. Where was spring? And why did its absence bother Jenny so much? Could it be that at long, dreaded last, Jenny West was finally becoming a Californian?

The idea made her shiver. For what was a Californian other than a person who had never learned the discipline of making hay while the sun shone. And continuing to muddle through even if it didn't. Being a midwesterner, she had learned early in life not to waste time waiting around for sunny days; she had learned not to let the weather become a sign post for her actions, her thoughts. If the snow was two feet deep, well, tough shit. Work still had to be done. If people were drowning in the streets, get out the boat. Time was a-wasting. And when that sun finally turned up after the long, hard winter—the joy, the joy! In the midwest people learned to be grateful for the damn little they got.

But Californians—they expected three hundred sixty-five days of sunshine per year and collapsed into sulks when they didn't get them. Or rather, the more realistic of them collapsed into sulks. The rest simply created an imaginary world of cloudless climes and starry skies; they became movie-makers.

Jenny's arms were strong now, her back straight. She could carry a tray loaded with beer mugs from one end of the Pink Pussy to the other without a whimper; she could listen to the most inane mutterings of inebriates with a smile. Jenny had developed grit.

Her flirtation with Mo sustained her. He came in every night and entertained her with readings from whatever book he was working on that week. "Jen, listen. How do you like this? *With a smile, he forced her to her knees, noticing all the while her dark, hungry eyes which longed so for his swollen cock. 'Beg for it,' he told her and she, eyes glazed with hunger, cried, 'Oh God! Give it to me! Give it to me!'*"

Jenny snickered. "Sounds like she's making it with God."

"Shut up, bitch and listen. *Unzipping his fly, he produced his gigantic cock and rubbed it slowly, tantalizingly across her forehead. Unable to control herself any longer, she grabbed it with both hands and thrust it, to the hairy hilt, into her mouth.*"

"Hey, wait. You said on page forty-three that he was twelve inches long. She couldn't do that!"

"Dummy. Didn't you see 'Deep Throat'?" He looked up at her with an expression of disgust.

"I don't go to the movies. But by the way, that reminds me of something. Why is it that men never accuse women of penis envy when they're trying to get a woman to gobble their cock? Why do they just say that when a woman is trying to do something for herself?"

Mo looked alarmed. "As the poet said, 'Ain't me, Babe. I-all is lib-er-a-ted.' " He put on his street talk. "No skin off me what women wants to do. No, mama! We all cousins under the privates."

Jenny smiled wickedly. "We'll see about that, Mo.

119

We'll just see about that."

She left him looking hopeful.

Wanda was in the dressing room filing down her nails. "They were starting to interfere with my typing," she explained.

"Still in the typing pool, eh?" Jenny asked, knowing that Wanda's doctoral dissertation was finished.

Wanda grinned. "Oh, I thought I had told you. The boss said the other day that as soon as I get my Ph. D. he'll promote me to secretary. That is, if I promise to learn shorthand."

"Congratulations."

"Yeah. It's very gratifying to have my patience, diligence, and hard work properly rewarded. Makes one believe in the system, it does."

Jenny laughed. "Yes, it does make one believe something about the American system, it sure does." She looked around. "Where's Janine? Isn't this supposed to be her shift?"

Wanda sighed. "Supposed to be. But she no-showed and Lance called me and told me to dance a double tonight. What the hell. He's paying me double. So what if it makes my tits fall off."

"Did Janine call?"

Wanda looked disgusted. "No, so old Lance drove over to her house after getting no answer on the phone. Thought she might be hurt or something."

"Lance did that?"

"Yeah. There's a nice person buried somewhere under all that shit. But anyway, he got over there and there was her husband sitting out on the front steps, crying. Janine had left him a note saying she'd run off to Tulsa, Oklahoma, with the mail carrier."

"Boy, that's tough. I feel sorry for her husband, poor thing."

"Oh, don't. He's in advertising. So, anyway, now we

120

need another dancer. But in the meantime, I'm going to clean up on overtime. Think I'll tell my boss at the office where to shove his typewriter."

They laughed.

The night was slow due to the continuing drizzle. Mrs. Wyzenski sat in her wheelchair drinking beer and scowling at the cash register. The only customer besides Mo was the man at the bar who kept doing unrecognizable imitations of movie stars. "Who's this?" He'd pluck at Jenny's sleeve as she tried to sneak past. "I'll bet you know who this is. This is perfect."

"Cary Grant," Jenny guessed desperately. "Gary Cooper. Clark Gable."

"Sidney Greenstreet," he said, accusingly. "Don't you know a perfect Sidney Greenstreet when you see one?"

Like a wind-up toy he continued, except that he seemed to have discovered the secret of perpetual motion. He wouldn't run down. On and on he went, doing one imitation after another until Jenny wanted to scream. "Watch this." He slinked and vamped and twisted his mouth. "Bette Davis!"

Near midnight he finally became so drunk that Lance had grounds to throw him out. "Let's close up early," he said, locking the door against the man who was still doing imitations on the sidewalk in the rain. "That guy was the straw that broke the camel's back."

Cheered by the prospect of going home early, Jenny answered, "Yeah. One rotten apple spoils the whole bunch, doesn't it?"

Mrs. Wyzenski snickered and Lance patted her arm in agreement. "Got a ride?"

Jenny looked back at the table where Mo was sitting. "Yeah. I've got one."

"Far out, baby. This place has real style." Mo had

driven Jenny home in his ragged clanking van.

Jenny laughed. "Yeah, Mo. In a way it does. I'm glad you appreciate it."

He had crossed back to her and his arm was around her waist. Jenny smiled with approval and anticipation.

"Yeah," Mo continued as his hand travelled northward. "Most women—they don't know what it is they want. They just sit around all the time, complaining because they don't have more of what they don't know they want. Women like you—you know what you're doing, where you're going. You don't have to suck up to anybody." He grinned. "Figure of speech."

Jenny smiled happily. "Figure of speech."

"Any man—he gets threatened about all this liberation—why he's just a damned fool. Doesn't know what's good for him. Cause all this liberation it's gonna take women off men's backs. Women gonna stop hassling their man to get this, do that, buy this. Cause women gonna be able to do all that themselves. Leave their man alone, then. Except in bed."

Jenny snuggled. "Right."

He turned off the light.

Mo left early, with profuse hugs and kisses. "I know you gotta work, Mama. But think about me." When Jenny heard a knock on the door later in the day, she thought he had returned. Smiling, she opened the door. It turned out to be Sushi and a flushed Angela. "Hey. It's happening!" Sushi beamed.

"What's happening?" inquired Jenny dumbly.

"The baby," said Angela. "I'm having contractions!" She was wearing a crash helmet; beyond her stood Sushi's Harley-Davidson at the curb.

"Baby?" Jenny squeaked in alarm. "The baby's coming? And you came here? To my studio? On your bike?"

"Oh, Jen," Angela sneered disdainfully. "The contractions are still fifteen minutes apart. We've got ages to go and we just got bored hanging around our place and timing them. We just jumped on the bike and came over to kill time."

"Jumped on the bike." Jenny wasn't dumb. She had read *Gone With the Wind* and all the other novels describing women in childbirth. One sure sign of labor, she knew, was loud screams. Sushi and Angela were putting her on. "Come on in," she said with a can't-fool-me smile. "Sit down and rest a spell."

"Thank you," Angela said formally, and entered and reclined regally (if ponderously) on the mattress. She propped herself up with the pillow and said, "Anyway. your place is a lot closer than ours to the hospital. We'll split when the contractions get to be five minutes apart."

Jenny decided to play along. "Gee. Five minutes? Aren't you cutting it a little close?"

"Nah," said Sushi, putting his helmet on the window ledge. "We timed it the other day and it's only four minutes from here. And that was during rush hour." He pulled a brightly-colored pinwheel from his jacket and took it to Angela. He propped it between two cushions so that it stood perkily.

"What the hell's that?" Jenny asked.

"Her focal point. It'll keep her mind from wandering. She's due for another contraction any time now."

It was at that point that Jenny began to get nervous.

Then, as Jenny watched fascinated, Angela began to go into an open-eyed trance, staring fixedly at the pinwheel drawing her breath in slowly, then finally releasing it even more slowly.

"Fine," Sushi said to her. "Relax. Loose and easy."

Jenny held her breath and she could hear Sushi's

watch tick. Angela seemed to be the only person breathing.

Then, as suddenly as it began, it was over and Angela sat up and smiled brightly. "Could I have some water?"

Jenny ran into the bathroom and fetched a dixie-cup full. "Here!" She shoved it at the girl so quickly that half of it spilled.

Sushi laughed. "Jen! Are you uptight?"

Angela grinned. "I'll bet your mother raised you on horror stories of childbirth."

"She did mention something about it hurting."

"Well, calm down," Sushi said. "You're so damn nervous you'll drive us all crazy." He was quiet for a moment, thinking, and then snapped his fingers. "I know! I'll go get us some alcoholic beverages. Loosen us up."

Startled, Jenny cried, "Hey! Don't leave me alone with her!"

Angela sneered. "Don't worry, Jen. It's not catching."

"Liquor store's just across the street. Won't take me a minute." And with that, Sushi went out the door.

There was silence. Total silence. Jenny looked at Angela. Angela looked at Jenny. Unable to stand it, Jenny inquired, "Got enough water?"

"Yeah."

"Well. Good."

"Right."

"Fine."

"Right."

They gave up and went back to staring at each other.

After what seemed like hours, Sushi bustled in with a bottle of sake, a bottle of tequila, some salt, and four lemons. "Thought we might as well do this up right," he explained. "A real celebration of life."

Hardly had he sat them down on the floor when Jenny had grabbed the tequila. She poured herself a dixie-cup full, cut a lemon into slices with her palette knife, and poured salt on the back of her wrist. She was all set to go. Bracing herself, she went. She slugged the tequila, bit the lemon, then licked the salt, giving a small shriek. "Aarrghh!"

"Boy, Jen. It really impresses me the way you drink that stuff," Sushi said admiringly. "I'm convulsed for two minutes after a shot like that."

Jenny smiled weakly but she was already feeling better.

Sushi, deciding that he wasn't really up to the occasion, sipped delicately at his sake. Angela lapped at her water. They all began to relax, and Sushi, for the first time, noticed the canvas Jenny was working on. "Wow. So that be honorable *Breasts.* Far out." He walked back several steps in order to get a better look at the entire composition. "That's a lot brighter than your usual stuff. Aren't most of the colors uncut?"

"Nah. It just looks that way, but I've neutralized everything a little except the nipples."

"Still, bet you have to wear shades while you're working on it."

Jenny grinned. "Just about. It is quite a departure from my usual stuff."

"I like it, Jen. I really do. Do you think it's going to mean something—in the development of your work? Think maybe you'll start using more color now?"

Jenny shook her head. "I don't know, Sushi. This painting may turn out to be just an isolated experience. It's pretty hard, you know, to paint a topless dancer in grays and browns. And I'm not too sure I want to do any more with that subject matter. It's too real."

"That's probably because you're around it three nights a week."

"Yeah."

"But still, I think you might be on to something."

They talked painting for a while until they were interrupted by a "for Christ's sake" from Angela.

Jenny looked over at her, saw that she wasn't having another contraction, but was sitting up glumly, staring at them. "What's the problem?" Jenny asked.

Sushi answered, "Aw, it's just the pregnancy. She can't stand to hear me talk shop—it irritates her. Thinks I should be thinking of nothing but the baby—since that's what she's doing."

"Piss on you," Angela snarled.

Jenny raised her eyebrows. Angela was usually Little Mary Sunshine. Butter wouldn't melt in her mouth.

Jenny changed the subject. "Say, folks. You're treating me—so let me treat you." She went to her paint stand and picked up a large, widemouthed jar labeled Transparent Glazing Gel. "Here," she handed it to Sushi.

"Oh, thanks, Jen, but I don't use acrylics."

"Open it, nit."

Sushi unscrewed the top, looked inside, and a big smile spread over his face. "Old girl, you have class." He fished out a packet of tinfoil and spread it open to reveal three joints.

Jenny explained, "I was saving them for the opening—but we might as well indulge right now."

"Far out," muttered a sunnier Angela.

Two hours later they were all stoned and Sushi and Jenny were drunk as well, Angela having declined the alcohol.

Sushi was winding up a story about his big show. "So there I was—among all those super-hips. I felt like the lone kamikaze. Say, did I tell you Dodd was queer?"

"No!" Jenny squeaked. "That fart made a grab at me!"

"Shit, woman. He just does that so nobody'll get

126

wise. He's been closeted so long he's got moths. I knew something was up when he asked me if Japanese boys were circumcised. Then he wanted to see."

They both giggled.

"Old bastard," said Jenny.

"Old shithead," said Sushi.

"Ass hole."

"Cocksucker." They both roared over that one.

A tiny voice from the corner said, "Hey, folks. I think it's time."

But Jenny and Sushi were flying, stoned out of their minds. "Who's that?" Sushi asked. "Oh, it's old Angela, Jenny. Says it's time." He poked Jenny hard in the ribs. She seemed to be dozing off.

She came to with a jerk. "Time? Time for what?"

"The baby, Angela says."

"Oh. The baby."

Unsteadily, they got to their feet. Angela was now propped up on only one pillow and was breathing in short pants.

"Oh, oh," said Sushi.

"Oh, oh what?" asked Jenny.

"That's transitional breathing."

Jenny giggled. "Transitional breathing, eh? Far out. What's that mean?"

"That it's time," Sushi giggled back.

"It means that I'm having the baby, you nerfs!" screamed Angela. "Get me to Cedars."

"She wants to go to the hospital," Sushi commented, then took another drag on his joint.

"Coward," tittered Jenny. "Always knew the girl was yellow." She and Sushi passed the joint back and forth.

After one last drag, Sushi said, "Well, old girl. Responsibility calls."

"The new Sushi," Jenny giggled.

Sushi went over to Angela and helped her to her feet.

"Oh! Ouch!" Angela protested. Sushi finally got her up and leaned her against the wall. "Every three minutes, Sushi," she gasped.

"Far out," he replied. "Guess I'd better start up the bike."

He went out the door slowly, still giggling. The bike started with a roar and Sushi yelled, "Your chariot a-waits, my lady." Slowly, ponderously, Angela wobbled toward the bike but halfway there she stopped and sat down on the sidewalk, breathing in rapid little pants again. Jenny remembered the pinwheel and rushed it to her, holding it in front of Angela's nose. Angela's eyes locked on it.

Sushi shut off the bike. "Wow. Far out. Labor on Beverly Boulevard."

Jenny laughed and took another drag. "I think it's going to be birth on Beverly Boulevard in a minute." They roared, and Jenny added, "Man, you're not going anywhere on that bike with her or the little bastard'll be born doing a headstand on the saddle seat. We'd better get a cab. Besides, cab drivers know all about birthin' babies."

Angela's rapid breathing stopped and she tried to get up. Jenny and Sushi helped her and they took her back into the studio. "Somebody do something," Angela bleated. "I think I'm going to have it right here!"

"Better not. Carlos would evict me for sure." Jenny convulsed with laughter over this witticism. "I doubt if he's covered for childbirth."

"Piggy's," Sushi said, with an air of having solved the problem.

"Piggies?" Jenny inquired blankly. "Ain't no hog belly 'round here."

"Nit!" But he giggled anyway. "Nah. There's always cabs over at Piggy's. Let's take her over there." He hauled Angela back out the door.

"I don't think I can make it," Angela gasped. They took her back inside and pushed her on the mattress. Once more in a comfortable position, she stopped yelling and started panting again.

"Holy shit!" Sushi looked at his watch. "Every two minutes!" He ran out the door, Jenny right behind him, leaving Angela alone. They ran across the street, dodging speeding cars, and ran into Piggie's parking lot.

Piggie's Palace was bravely lit. It was round and had more flying buttresses than Notre Dame. Upon each buttress (painted orange) were mud-colored ceramic plaques of various edibles—bread, oranges, sausages, chickens, hamburgers. The building proper was purple with lime green trim. Atop revolved a huge pink pig.

Piggie's Palace was a coffee shop.

Two cabs were parked in the lot and Jenny and Sushi ran toward them, yelling in unison, "Taxi! Emergency!"

The drivers were leaning on the doors of their yellow steeds, chatting. The eldest, a plump cheerful type, said, "Where did you have in mind to go? I'm off duty."

"Hospital. Going to have a baby. Cedars."

"Potheads," the driver said laconically, climbed in his cab and took off.

This left the younger driver, bearded and long-haired. Jenny figured he would be more sympathetic. "Please," she pleaded. "She's back at my place, across the street. She couldn't walk over here. It's desparate."

"How far apart are the pains?" he questioned.

"Contractions," contradicted Sushi. "Two minutes."

The cabbie looked alarmed. "Two minutes? Mister, you'd better start boiling water. You're not going anywhere in this cab. Ever seen what afterbirth does to upholstery?" He opened the door and got in. Leaning his head out of the window, he added, "Besides. I've got a call in Watts." With that, he sped off.

"Bastards," raged Jenny, the shock having brought her back to earth. "Dirty mother-fucking bastards!" She and Sushi looked at each other. "We can't let her have it at my place, for Christ's sake."

"Why not?" Sushi giggled. "You're a woman. Supposed to know all about birthin' babies."

"Fuck you," snarled Jenny, all good humor gone. "Straighten up. Inhale. Deep breaths."

"Why? I'm not in labor." Sushi smiled blissfully at the revolving pink pig.

Leaving him there, Jenny ran into Piggie's and headed for the pay phone. She called Lou, then collected Sushi and got him back across the street.

Lou arrived almost immediately, driving Silver's Rolls Royce with the reluctant Silver in back. "Here," Lou said, emerging from the cavernous interior. "I've had Silver fix up the back with clean sheets and towels. Just in case."

Silver looked morosely at them. "Pot. I smell pot."

Jenny gave him the finger and followed Lou into the studio where Angela lay on the mattress, her face dripping with perspiration. The rapid panting had become almost inaudible, and her hands roamed in swift, small circles over her protruding abdomen. It seemed to Jenny that the bulge was lower than before.

"Angie," Lou said, leaning over her. "We're taking you to the hospital now."

"No. No." She stopped the motion of her hands and pointed towards her feet.

They all looked. Angela had taken off her slacks and underpants. They were lying by the side of the mattress, wet. The mattress was soaked.

"Oh, dear," Lou said. "Her water's broken."

"Her what has what?" Jenny asked.

Ignoring her, Lou continued, "And the baby's already crowning. We can't possibly move her."

130

There was a long silence, broken finally by a weak, "Oh, shit." Jenny's worst fears were coming true.

"Go get Silver," Lou snapped. "And the sheet and towels. This bed's enough to give her gangrene."

Silver came into the studio, white as the sheet he was carrying. "For God's sake, Lou! Not here. Not in this opium den. You don't know anything about delivering babies!"

"Of course I do," Lou retorted. "I've seen over three hundred babies delivered. By the best doctors in the country. Gannon. Kildare. Marcus Welby. I could do it blindfolded."

Jenny looked at Silver's horrified face, Lou's rolled up sleeves, Angela's straining face, and walked over to the corner where Sushi sat smiling vacantly. "Hit me," she said.

So Sushi passed the joint.

She couldn't look—hid, instead, her face in her hands—but the sounds told her more than she had ever really wanted to know. Angela growled like a dog, grunted like a rooting pig, but she never screamed. Perhaps that was the worst of it—that the expected never happened.

Shortly, after an unusually prolonged growl, came a bubbling cough and a cry.

"It's a boy!" cried Lou.

"Far out," said Sushi.

"Jesus," said Jenny.

"Where's my valium?" asked Silver.

"She shouldn't ought to have done it." Sushi complained ungrammatically, if feelingly, four days later. "Shouldn't oughta." George McGovern Takamoto wriggled angrily in his arms. He didn't like his distant, absent mother spoken of in such harsh terms.

Jenny shrugged her shoulders and looked a-round Sushi's pad. All the frilly accoutrements were gone—left was the bare, stark, Japanese decor. Upon release from the hospital, Angela had left, taking all her "True Romances" and copies of "The Rolling Stone" with her. "So what does 'should' have to do with anything in life?" Jenny asked rhetorically. "Hitler shouldn't have killed all those Jews and Nixon shouldn't have called Helen Gahagan Douglas a communist, either. But they did. And Angela did. However . . ." Jenny paused for emphasis, "there seems to be some sort of comic justice that works in these things. You just watch. Some day old Angela will get hers. She'll probably find that doctor, marry him, have swarms of children, and be abandoned for a golf cart."

Sushi stuck the bottle (scientific nurser—most like Mama) in George McGovern's mouth and continued his plaint. "After all I did for her. And now look at me. Alone. An unwed father."

Jenny tsked-tsked as she saw a damp stain spreading on Sushi's knees where George was cradled.

"Women," Sushi continued to whine, oblivious of his soggy state. "I'll never understand them. All that talk Angela spouted about how beautiful motherhood was and then the next thing you know, I'm left holding the baby. Where's the sense in that?"

Jenny shrugged. "Well, none of those pink frilly dresses she bought would be right for George, you know. And the one thing our Angela has always been is a realist. And besides, she told me that she never liked her Ken doll very much. There wasn't anything creative she could do with his hair."

Although emotionally exhausted, Jenny managed to finish *Breasts* the next day. It had taken her a month longer, almost twice the time she usually spent on a painting, but, surveying it, she knew it was worth every minute. She sat staring at the drying acrylic, a once flat, two-dimensional object that was now alive and singing because of her hand. Raw and vulgar it was but it had that special magic that could never be quite planned or consciously carried out. It was the culmination of her months of work and it was magnificent.

There are few moments in life so definitive that a person can say, "All right, this is it. A finished journey. A completion. Tomorrow I'll start off from here, but as for the past—it's over."

Jenny understood the Book of Genesis as few could. (After all, she had a midwestern upbringing and had been hauled along to church every Sunday.) God created Heaven and Earth and saw that it was good and Jenny knew how he felt. Exactly. Maybe her creations—her paintings—couldn't talk to her like God's did to him, but they couldn't give her any trouble, either. So it balanced out.

An idea occurred to her. Was it possible that most men's almost maniacal belief in the sacredness of motherhood had something to do with stifled creativity? They had somehow developed the idea (based, like many ideas, on envy) that women's desire to fulfill their own creative urge was adequately serviced by childbirth. That was what men wanted to believe. For ages men (and some women who were more akin to parrots than human beings) insisted that biology was creativity, at least where women were concerned. Jenny couldn't hate them for it although their insistence and adherence to an old, outdated idea had crippled her own life. No, she couldn't really blame them. After all things were rough all over.

There was a book she had read once, a funny, odd book with no paragraphs and little punctuation which had raised an interesting point. In it, a man said to a woman, "I want your body." And the woman replied, "You can have it when I'm through with it." Jenny admired the independence of that remark but thought that the author hadn't taken it quite far enough. If all anybody ever wanted was just your body, why then everything would be all sweetness and light. Hell, a little screwing never killed anyone and it could burn calories, too. The trouble was that men wanted so much more than just a woman's body; they wanted her mind, her will, her soul. And what snappy remark could you make to that?

Jenny sighed (as she usually did whenever she thought about woman's fate) and began the final clean-up. She'd love to take a vacation, visit old friends, maybe visit her old art school and see how things were going. She wondered if the school still held their life drawing classes in the muggy, windowless basement.

Jenny smiled at the memory. How far she had come from those early days.

Life drawing had been her favorite class. The twisted, oiled bodies of the models were endlessly fascinating in their variety. Some models had long, smooth bodies, some had tight knots of muscles straining against a thin covering of flesh—no two were ever the same.

Jenny never thought of the models as human beings; they were merely packages of muscle and bone to her, shapes to draw, to paint. The only day she had been aware of a model's humanity was the day one—a male— had dropped his dressing gown and revealed bulging genitals encased in a white cotton pouch. It turned Jenny's stomach. That peculiar, sanitary whiteness was horrifying, as if the wearer considered his body a dirty thing that needed to be tidied up.

She had learned early that there was something sexless and endlessly innocent about a naked body. Jenny—who could hardly look at a handsome man without experiencing some degree of lust—was completely unmoved by a naked man. "Let it all hang out," the saying said, but when it did, it left Jenny cold.

She had discussed this with her fellow and sister students and found that it was a common syndrome. A bearded sculptor had told her about the time a female model had kept on her earrings and he had had to rush to the school lavatory to relieve his erection. The odd thing was, he told her, that he had used the woman as a model for six months and found her distinctly unappealing to him. Until the day of the earrings.

Having cleaned the studio to a rare, spotless perfection, there was nothing left for Jenny to do. She decided that she might as well get drunk but God only knew if it would be a celebration or a wake. Splurging for once, she bought a bottle of Scotch at the liquor store next to Piggy's, then called Pearce.

"This it, then?" Pearce asked, as he supervised the loading of the last painting in his van. "What about that?" he pointed to *Breasts*.

"I'll bring it by myself tomorrow," she said. "I just finished it today and I want it to dry a little."

There was a small sound from Pearce—something like *eekk!*

"It's acrylic," Jenny said dryly. "It'll be dry in two days. That's just a glaze on top." Jenny was still furious with Pearce for the wording on the flyer but she knew there was no point in bringing it up. He would just quote a line of dribble about business being business, and talk to her like she was a naive, spoiled child. Pearce, like most art dealers, found it almost impossible to treat his artists as adults.

As usual, Jenny found refuge in cynicism.

"Great flyer," she said.

"Glad you like it."

"Yeah."

Pearce slid his oily eyes toward her and other than that did not seem to notice her tone. "Chopped liver or chicken salad?" he asked.

"Chopped liver." She had come up in the world. Refreshments were now being served at her showings.

When Pearce left, Jenny sat down in the corner, her blanket wrapped around her, her bottle of Scotch raised in a toast. "L'aichem," she said to *Breasts.*

Jenny awoke the next morning thinking her mouth had grown hair overnight. Her head, of course, was killing her.

But there was also a new sensation, one of dampness. She was wet. The first thought to cross her mind was that she had (shame shame) wet her pants while drunkenly asleep. According to her mother, she had been an incorrigible bed-wetter well into her ninth year. Godalmighty, she had had a relapse. But how? She'd been drunk before and this had never happened. And she hadn't eaten any watermelon (no doubt that was the real reason behind the usual white prejudice of Blacks—not so much the idea that Blacks were mentally inferior and morally loose, but a deep, dark suspicion that they were bed-wetters. All that watermelon, you know.)

Slowly, guiltily, Jenny began to rise. Then she noticed that her arms, also, were wet. Her neck. Her hair. Everything. She looked around and saw that her entire studio floor was under four inches of water—and she knew that she hadn't had that much Scotch.

136

She experienced a tremendous urge to relieve her full, innocent bladder.

Barefoot, dripping, she splashed to the toilet. As she sat there on her porcelain throne, she surveyed the sea before her. In its way, it was quite exotic—a gentle current emanated from the door, and swirled around the easel. A lovely reddish gray in color—a neutralized, cut-back burnt sienna. Approaching burnt umber.

Jenny flushed the toilet and splashed back across the room, finding a perch on her stool—the highest point. *Breasts* was all right. It was secured to the easel, above the water line by at least two feet and in no immediate danger, although the water appeared to be rising.

Fortunately for Jenny, her clothes were on hangers and she managed to get dressed while balancing on the window ledge. She didn't bother with shoes.

It occurred to her to find out what had happened. It was quite possible that there had been another earthquake (she always slept through them) and California, at long predicted last, had broken away and was now adrift somewhere in the Pacific. If so, she hoped they would make it to Tahiti. She had always enjoyed Polynesian food.

Getting the door open wasn't easy. The water had swollen the wood and it was stuck tight, but after much pounding, kicking, and cursing, it finally groaned open.

More water rushed in. The street was flooded.

Well, it had to happen some time. All that rain and no place to go, except to the lowest point. It was really too bad there were no storm drains. She wiggled her toes in the current for awhile and then decided to call Carlos. No doubt he was covered for floods and a quick look through the closet while she was getting her clothes had shown her what water could do to encyclopedias. And hotplates.

Besides, he might have sustained enough damage to the building itself to collect on his own. She looked across the street at Piggy's Palace, high and dry on its mountain of concrete. The water stretched up and down the street as far as the eye could see so Jenny had no recourse other than to step off the curb and wade right in.

There was an orange Volkswagen in the middle of the street, its driver sitting on the roof smoking a cigarette. "Wanna screw?" he asked as Jenny paddled past. Shaking her head in the negative, she kept paddling. Maybe later, she thought, admiring his savoir faire.

She finally washed up on the other side of the street and crawled up on the curb, somehow, without falling. A man's hat drifted slowly by and Jenny looked around nervously to see if a body came with it. There was nothing—except the Volkswagen, its amorous driver and two apricot-colored poodles with rhinestone collars. She shook her head sadly at them. The water was playing hell with their set.

On dry ground in the parking lot, Jenny shook herself and tried to wring out her levis, but she gave it up as a lost cause. The rain was still coming down and was resaturating everything. A yip from one of the poodles attracted her attention and she saw it swimming around a red Mustang which had just joined the Volkswagen. Both drivers were chatting amiably.

Piggy's was bravely lit, courage in the face of adversity, the California spirit. She could see the blue uniformed waitresses inside standing immaculate, immobile, and deaf to the cries of emaciated, swollen-bellied customers. Those worthy ladies polished ashtrays, straightened toothpicks, rearranged plastic flowers, and kept themselves much too busy for anything so mundane as serving customers.

The pay phone was inside on a wall rack in the lobby,

138

so Jenny went through the large glass doors (they informed her again that Piggy's accepted BankAmericard, Master Charge, and Diners Club) and made it half way to the phone when she heard a high, stern voice, "No shoes, no service."

Jenny looked at her bare feet.

A waitress, tall and with the thin, parched looks of Pat Nixon, repeated her command, "No shoes, no service."

"I just wanted to use the phone," Jenny explained. "My place is flooded and I have to call my landlord."

"No shoes, no service." The bubble hairdo trembled with superiority.

"Hey, lady, your needle's stuck. I don't want service, I want the phone." Jenny was becoming angry.

"No shoes, no service," the pale blue eyes sparkled with power.

"Fuck you," Jenny hissed as she finally faced defeat. She went back out into the street.

There were three cars, now, in the middle of the street, and all the drivers were huddled together on top of the Mustang, throwing dice and having a merry time. Jenny heard one call out, "Seven-eleven, Mama needs platform shoes!"

As she waded in again, the poodles swam up to her and followed her all the way to her studio, swimming alongside and nipping at her hands. By the time she reached her door a fight had started among the crap shooters and one of them had pulled a knife.

Inside, Jenny got her waterlogged sneakers out of the closet, put them on (which took at least eight minutes) and went back to the curb. The poodles were waiting for her. They followed her back past the wallowing cars where the man with the knife had cut himself and was dripping blood into the street. The other two drivers were arguing about where to place the tourniquet.

139

This time, Jenny's entrance at Piggy's was unheralded and she got to the pay phone without argument although she left huge, sloshing puddles on the purple and red carpet. Carlos was home and he grew hysterical at the word damage. He told her that he'd be over right away with his insurance man.

Jenny also called Lou, Sushi, and Mo. She needed a little help from her friends.

Fording the street again she looked for the poodles, then saw them perched on an uprooted palm tree which was slowly floating west towards Beverly Hills. There was an L. A. P. D. black and white parked near the other cars. The two policemen sat on their roof playing cards. As Jenny went past, one called out, "Wanna screw?"

Sushi arrived first with a slobbering George McGovern tucked safely inside a basket and chewing toothlessly on a finger. Sushi put him on the window ledge where he chewed happily away.

"Shit, what a mess," Sushi commented. "I brought a mop with me but I don't think it'll do you any good. What you need is a bucket to bail out with. Looks like you'll sink any minute." Mo arrived soon afterwards shaking his head and saying, "It looks, Mama, like you're paying for your sins."

When Lou got there, they were sitting on the window ledge with a cooing George McGovern and smoking a joint. Lou turned out to be the most realistic of the group—she had brought buckets, rags, and sponges. "Used to have a dingy in Minnesota," she explained. "Also got the tv in the car. Thought we'd watch the special report."

"What special report?" asked Jenny, wondering idly if they would be electrocuted when Lou plugged in.

"Oh, it's like this all over, you know. Not just here. Houses are starting to slide off the hills again and this time the camera crews are all out covering it."

"Far out," approved Sushi, who had never seen a house slide off a hill.

Carlos arrived then, near tears and trailing a thin, resigned insurance man. "I've told you, Mr. Conejo," the insurance man was saying. "This particular act of God is not covered by your policy."

"Then I'll sue that neeger mayor. For damagees!" He cast a panicked look at Mo, who was grinning from ear to ear. "Sorry," he muttered. Carlos's usually immaculate elegance was damp and rain spattered. "Oh, my beautiful, beautiful building. What have they been doing to you?" He sloshed through the studio, his tears adding to the increasing flood. "Ruined! All ruined! The work of a lifetime. All my dreams! All my hopes! In ashes!"

"In puddles," a giggling Sushi corrected.

The insurance man sat down on Jenny's stool and took out a pack of cigarettes. "Smoke?" he asked.

"Thanks anyway, but we've got our own," Jenny answered, waving a joint at him.

"Yes. Well." He looked determinedly away from them.

In the bathroom Carlos was trying to flush the toilet. "Broke again!" he wept. "Jesus, Mary and Joseph! Why me, God? Why me? I only go to Latin masses!"

Lou had given up bailing. "It's hopeless," she said to Jenny. "The water's coming back in as fast as we throw it out. You're just going to have to move in with me until it stops raining."

At that, Carlos rushed from the bathroom, leaving a wake behind him like a speeding motorboat. "Permanent," he screamed. "You're moving permanent!" His accent had entirely disappeared. "This is it! Evicted!" He pointed a jeweled finger at Jenny. "You! Out! No

141

more tenants, no more pot heads, no more insurance problems! I'm selling out!"

Jenny gasped, "You can't do that. I've got a lease. I've been here for five years!"

"Four and a half," Carlos sneered, "and yes I can. Piggy wants to expand his parking lot and offered me sixty thousand dollars for this property. You fight it and I'll have it declared eminent domain."

"That's illegal," Jenny cried, casting anguished glances at her friends.

"Anything to do with parking lots is legal in Los Angeles," Mo observed.

With a smile of triumph, Carlos sailed out, the insurance agent in tow, congratulating him on his wise decision.

"Jen, you can move in with me," Sushi suggested. "My studio's big enough for the two of us."

"Same here," said Mo hopefully. "Got plenty of room."

Jenny sat on her stool, not quite successful in fighting back tears. "Thanks. Thanks." She started to cry in loud, slopping gulps.

Lou, always fine in the difficult moments of life, got the tiny portable tv up on the dry window ledge and turned it on. "Look, Jen," she said. "See, you're not the only one."

And it was true. On the tube was truly a tragic scene. The camera crews were up in posh Trousdale Estates surrounded by marble pillars and gilded birdbaths. Three large homes were listing dramatically on the hillside and a fourth seemed determined to salom to Sunset Boulevard. It was creeping forward slowly. Women wearing full length chinchillas, sables, leopards, and other dead animals scurried past the cameras carrying spilling jewelry boxes.

"Yes folks, a terrible tragedy is happening before

our very eyes," the newscaster intoned dramatically. "These beautiful homes—the pride of Los Angeles—are surely doomed along with their great and beautiful treasures they have so protectively embraced."

There came a sound of retching from Sushi and Mo.

The announcer continued, "But these people—the beautiful, the courageous—they hold their heads high and look toward the future with unbroken spirit." More people scurried past the camera. A Rolls Royce crept by laden with antiques, paintings, furs, poodles, and Lhasha Apsos.

"Yes, the heart of Los Angeles is here. The spirit of our people—the spirit that says, Come flood, come fire, come earthquake and Santana wind, we will face up to the elements with courage in our hearts and a smile on our lips."

Here he turned to a squat little man who was waddling by with a Picasso under one arm and a Jasper Johns under the other. "Tell me, sir." The announcer pointed the microphone towards him, "What are your plans? What will you do now that your beloved home is gone?"

Blinking puffy eyes in the rain the little man said, "Live on my yacht, I guess. Too bad it's all the way down in Newport."

"Ah, sir, but these are trying times."

"You're right there. But what the hell. The Rolls can do one-twenty on the freeways. But I think I'll use the Ferrari. Because of the gas shortage." He walked off toward his waiting Bentley.

"Never thinking of themselves, even in times of crisis. The spirit of the pioneer. The spirit of the Angeleno. This is Duvall Heartshank for KQTZ—reporting live, once again, in the midst of history." In the background another home slid out of sight.

"Shee-it," breathed Mo in awe.

"The rats deserting their ships," said Jenny bitterly.

"Hey. Wait!" Lou's voice rose to a shriek. "Look!"

Crossing to the left of the screen was a familiar figure dressed in a pearl gray jumpsuit, clutching an Oscar in one hand and a stack of scripts in the other.

It was Silver.

"Silver takes too goddamn long in the john," Jenny complained as she wolfed down a plate of bacon and eggs. "I just about piss my pants every morning."

Lou gave her a fierce look. "Then get up earlier and beat him to it."

It had been a long week. Lou glumly surveyed her apartment which had begun to look like an American Red Cross emergency shelter. The den had become Jenny's headquarters. Her easel, acrylics, oils, and all the artifacts which artists are prone to drag around with them lay in a pile on the floor. The air was thick with the smell of turpentine and linseed oil.

The air was also thick with tension.

Silver was headquartered in Lou's bedroom. The wreck of his marbled palace had also signaled the wreck of his marriage; his wife had flown to Europe with the children, and he had flown into the arms of a sympathetic cooing Lou. He and Jenny had arrived at Lou's apartment at the same time, both drenched, dripping, shoving, and angry. Only the cannabis-mellowed intervention of Sushi prevented the two from coming to blows. Silver now rested beneath the mirrored ceiling, pondering his situation. Silk underwear, velvet jumpsuits, slave bracelets, and scripts were scattered around him. The Oscar sulked in the corner on a crocheted doily.

"Why couldn't he get a motel room?" Jenny said,

through a mouth filled with scrambled eggs.

"Why couldn't you?" Lou snapped back. Her temper was getting short due to the constant strain of mediating battles between the two.

"No money," Jenny said as if that explained all. The rich should succor the poor, was her philosophy. They should especially succor Jenny West.

"There's always welfare."

"You don't really mean that," said Jenny sanguinely, buttering another piece of toast. "Why, the paintings I've given you alone would pay my rent here for the next six months."

Lou sat in silence. As always, it was touche for Jenny. She never pulled her punches—and never hesitated to even scores. Controlling her temper, Lou managed to say, "Have you looked for another place yet? I saw an empty storefront on Normandie yesterday. It looked pretty good."

Jenny looked up. "Good or cheap?"

Lou sighed. "Cheap."

"Beggars can't be choosers," growled Silver, entering the kitchen. He sat down at the table, looking pointedly away from Jenny.

"I've got exactly forty-three dollars and fifty-seven cents to do my choosing with, smart ass," Jenny snapped.

"Jenny, go take your bath. Now," ordered Lou.

The air was still except for heavy breathing. Then Jenny got up and without another word went into the bathroom.

When she emerged, half an hour later, powdered and perfumed at Lou's expense, Silver had left to go to the studio and Lou was washing the dishes. Not wishing to push her luck any further, Jenny picked up a dish towel and joined her at the sink.

"How the mighty are fallen," Lou observed cynically as Jenny wiped ineffectually at a plate.

"Just trying to pull my share of the load," Jenny proclaimed self-righteously.

"That'll be the day."

They stood together, washing and rinsing, wiping and stacking. Jenny avoided looking at the dishwater, preferring instead the translucent gleam of clean china.

"You're not polishing silver, you know," Lou said as she noticed the fierce way Jenny had started drying the plates. "A whisk and a flick will do."

"I'm a perfectionist," Jenny said.

Lou shrugged her shoulders and handed Jenny the last plate. "Well, that's it. All done. I'll put them away."

Jenny fell back gratefully from the sink and watched as Lou carefully put the plates into their proper niches and hung the cups on their little hooks. "There," Lou sighed in satisfaction. "And thanks."

"Don't mention it," Jenny said, sitting down at the table. Lou poured them each a cup of coffee.

"So what are you going to do today?" Lou asked.

Jenny sighed. "Well, for one thing, I guess I'll tell them down at the Pink Pussy that I'm quitting."

"Ah."

Jenny sighed again, a little more loudly, a little more tremulously. "Pearce says he wants me to help hang the paintings. I'm just not going to be able to work down there any more." Jenny shook her head. "Besides, I've had it with cigarette smoke and beer fumes. They're hardly conducive to creative thought."

"I'm surprised you lasted as long as you did."

Jenny laughed. "To tell the truth, so am I."

The Pink Pussy was quiet that night. The rain had stopped and the sun had actually come out twice that day. The Californians had their hopes up again, and with renewed optimism came renewed sanding and varnishing of surfboards. They were home, busy. The sun would shine tomorrow. They knew it.

Jenny sat, more sadly than she would have believed, in the office with Lance and Mrs. Wyzenski.

"God helps those who help themselves, I always say," said Lance. "And anyway, we won't have any trouble replacing you."

"Oh, I wouldn't say that," barked Mrs. Wyzenski. "Jenny's one of a kind." She sniffed. "However, there are plenty of other starving young beauties out there. They'll all be showing up here the minute we put the Help Wanted sign in the window." She patted Jenny's arm. "We're invited to your opening, aren't we, dear?"

Jenny promised to send them all an invitation, and they parted amicably, Mrs. Wyzenski wheeling her chair close to give Jenny a farewell hug. Even Wanda seemed damp-eyed as she waved goodbye, her breasts bobbing to the music. Once outside the Pink Pussy, Jenny looked back. "Come on in. Four Koy Kittens." Resisting an impulse to meow, she walked away.

While she had been inside, it had finally happened. The rain had stopped. The sun was out.

The sun shone; it filtered softly through the smog and lay in golden sheets upon the concrete parking lots. People were streaming out of their apartments, surf-boards under their arms. They had already convinced themselves that the past few weeks had been merely a bad dream; it never rained in California.

Jenny drifted that day among those golden people, the milk-fed Californians. She had nowhere to go, nothing of any importance to do. Homeless and aimless, she walked the streets. She fed ducks at MacArthur Park, rode the fume-filled bus to the county museum and stared morosely at the LaBrea tar pits. She knew what it must have felt like being the last mastadon.

It was all over—the struggle which marked the finish of each painting. Left was only Jenny, an empty, pur-

147

poseless Jenny.

That night, sitting in the art room of the public library, Jenny was gripped by a fear so violent, so strong that she had to run to the women's restroom. She was shaking and heaving. The walls closed in on her. Still retching, she stumbled out into the heavy air. Looking up, she saw the bright neon sign on Aimee Semple McPherson's temple.

"Jesus Saves."

The day of the opening the sun was still out. Jenny was tempted to take it as an omen that her work would sell and she would become rich and famous, but she had been around too long. Omens were for quaking shepherds, not artists.

The reception was planned for seven-thirty. Pearce had promised to lay on some champagne, some celery, and chopped liver so the condemned woman could eat a hearty meal.

The big moment had finally arrived but Jenny felt nothing except the sinking weight of apathy. She sat on Lou's couch as Lou fussed with one set of false eyelashes after another, muttering, "Too spikey, too blatant, too wispy."

"God, Lou," Jenny said in exasperation. "This is just a preview for friends, not the opening night for one of Stirling's stinkers. Ain't gonna be nobody there but just us chickens."

But Lou kept on applying makeup. Finally getting the chosen set of eyelashes in place, she started on lipstick— first a pink, then an orangey-red. "Do I look all right?"

"Christ, you look fine," Jenny said wearily. "What difference does it make?"

Lou blinked at Jenny and one eyelash fell off. "Damn," she muttered, getting down on her knees and peering under the chair where it had drifted. "Rockets can go to the moon and back but nobody's come up with a good eyelash glue." Having found the eyelash, she glared up at Jenny. "It wouldn't kill you to fix up a little. The biggest night in your life and you look like that!"

Jenny looked hurt. *That* referred to her usual uniform of turtleneck and levis. "I've got on some new sandals," she said, pained. "And what the hell do you mean, biggest night in my life? Ha!"

Lou jumped nervously and reapplied the eyelash.

Jenny poured another dollop of Silver's Chivas Regal. It was all out of her hands, so there was no point in falling apart. The exhibit would start off just fine. All of her friends would be there along with every bus driver who had ever wished her a good day and every customer from the Pink Pussy who had never tried to pinch her. None of them had any money but they had bodies and would fill Pearce's small gallery. Jenny knew that nothing was more dismal than an under-populated reception—it stank of failure.

Not that tonight would be a resounding success, of course. She would probably sell four or five paintings at the posted price, and as the month wore on, would come down fifty percent on each painting. History invariably repeated itself.

But she didn't give a shit. All she wanted was enough money to restock her dwindling art supplies. Spring had sprung and she would be off to Disneyland to do some pastel portraits at six dollars a head.

Thinking about that, she poured herself another drink.

"I wish you'd straighten up, Jenny," Lou said as

she continued to work on her face.

Jenny laughed nastily. "I'm as straight as I ever want to be." The Scotch burned as, no doubt, did the flames of hell. "By the way, where's His Highness? Odd time to run an errand, isn't it? Just before we're supposed to leave?"

Lou blushed. "He wanted to pick up a friend."

Jenny shrugged. The more the merrier—as Lance would surely say.

About fifteen minutes later, as Lou was trying on her eighth shade of lipstick, voices in the hall announced Silver's return. The door opened and he padded in trailed by a tall, thin man with a dusting of freckles across his nose.

"One of your movie friends?" Jenny inquired, feeling high and nasty. "Another porn producer?"

The tall man blinked, "Not really—although I do confess to being a writer."

Stirling Silver smiled a cat/canary smile. "Let me introduce you two. Jenny, this is Haggis Selfright. The man who writes the art column for the *L. A. Journal*." He leaned back and watched Jenny's reaction, then satisfied, continued. "Haggie and I went to UCLA together. Didn't I ever tell you?"

"No," Jenny squeaked. "You never did. Pleasedtameecha." She picked up the Chivas for a final swig, straight from the bottle.

Haggis Selfright smiled blandly and said, "Shall we go? After your showing (which I'm sure will be charming) I am expected in Beverly Hills where there is a Picasso retrospective. All of my dear friends have kindly loaned their paintings for this tribute to the master."

Jenny's shock was wearing off and her mind was racing. What was this? Did Silver think her so devoid of talent that he pulled his strings just to see her get put down in print? UCLA friendships not withstanding,

Silver must know where Selfright's bodies were buried because it was common knowledge that Selfright never reviewed paintings—only "events" and "happenings." And even those had to have the freak's stamp of approval in order to draw him from his rarified tower. Unless word had it that an artist was going to disembowel his mother in a hand-carved casket, Selfright considered it too, too dull for words. Originality was his battle cry, his key word—and by his definition, vomit under glass was more original than daubs on canvas. After all, nature never repeated herself whereas people, alas, did.

"Lou," Jenny whispered. "Can I borrow some lipstick?"

They were the last of the crowd to arrive; most of her friends were already there, glasses of champagne in their hands, tipsy smiles on their faces. There was a scent of grass in the air. Sushi, George McGovern, Mo, Lance, Mrs. Wyzenski, Bert, and the others from Harold's, a waitress from Piggy's, the boys from the Balle aynd Tyte, Wanda Orlando, guards from the museum, and various bus drivers. A democratic crowd.

"Hail to the conquering hero!" cheered Sushi, glass raised and a stalk of celery hanging from his lip. Everybody cheered—and Jenny steeled herself to receive the embraces of her friends.

By the end of the evening she had sold three paintings. Lou bought *Danse Macabre*, Sushi bought *Breasts*, and Bert and Mo had gone in on one together and were busy making arrangements for it to hang one month in Mo's place, one month at Bert's. Several other sales looked likely. The janitor at the laundromat was discussing with his wife how much they would be able to afford per month on a small oil and a bus driver kept

151

returning coveteously to an acrylic. Ken's face was conspicuous for its absence—although he had been sent an invitation.

Jenny was a little drunk. Seeing her paintings together on the gallery walls had more than made up for the months of frustrations and disappointments. It could have been embarrassing, exhibiting the bare corners of her soul, but instead it was exhilirating. Jenny had seen her devils and met them head on. By painting them they were exorcised. They might come back on her again but she would keep painting them away—and there was nothing that could compare with that.

Jenny looked at her work with pride. It wasn't perfect—not one of her paintings could lay claim to perfection. One had too much red, it was unbalanced; another was so completely balanced it verged on the static; but still, they worked.

"It's good, Jen, really good," Sushi said, his arm around her. "It's so good that it's almost impossible to tell what you should have done and what you shouldn't have done."

Jenny hugged him. "Thanks, Sushi. Praise from my peers is almost as good as money from the masses."

He smiled drunkenly at her. "Have you ever thought about us getting married?"

Jenny laughed, kissed his cheek, and said, "And spoil a beautiful friendship? No, Sushi—but I'll be godmother to George McGovern."

George McGovern screamed in outrage at this heresy. It finally occurred to Jenny to look for Haggis Selfright. She wondered how he would look. Enigmatic or damning? Silver passed by on the way to the champagne and Jenny grabbed his arm. "Where's our Haggie?" she asked.

"Gone to Beverly Hills," said Silver. "The Blue Period

awaits."

Jenny couldn't help but look disappointed. "He sure didn't stay long."

"Never does," Silver explained. "He's known for having the quickest judgment in the West."

"Also the sloppiest," Jenny muttered so he could hear her.

Silver started to walk off, then turned around and said, "Uh, Jen. I didn't invite him so that he'd put you down. Really. Do you believe that?"

Jenny smiled at him. "You may be a prick, Silver— but I know you're not a liar."

Silver blushed at this backhanded compliment and went to join Lou.

Jenny stood looking after him. Well, who knew what good could lurk in the hearts of men? Old Silver had been trying to do her a favor, which was all right with her. It wasn't his fault that Selfright didn't like painting. Few critics did.

The noise was rising as the level of the bottles dropped and Jenny plunged back into the din.

Almost as many superlatives have been written about hangovers as about unrequited love but the next morning Jenny knew beyond a doubt that her hangover set some kind of a record. She couldn't find one portion of her anatomy that didn't hurt; her head, her eyes, her nose, her teeth, her fingernails—everything was throbbing and pulsing in ghastly concert and her stomach was heaving right along in time. She knew she was going to be sick but as she lay on Lou's daybed in the den, Jenny feared that the very act of rising would trigger her retch mechanism.

153

So she lay there reflecting on her sins. It hadn't been last night's reception so much that had contributed to her wretched state, but rather the bar-hopping which had followed. After hitting most of the bars on the Strip they had all wound up at the Pink Pussy, guzzling at Mrs. Wyzenski's expense, while little George McGovern babbled happily on the mirrored stage.

Jenny rolled her eyes toward the door, wincing slightly at the pain that action created. She was going to have to get up, going to have to make it to the bathroom—she couldn't lie there and wait until she eventually vomited from a prone position. That was how Jimi Hendrix had died.

With a final shudder, Jenny lurched off.

Fifteen minutes later she emerged from the bathroom, white, shaken, but certain in the knowledge that she would, after all, survive to drink again. It would take more than a measly little hangover to keep Jennifer Louise West down. She could smell bacon frying, coffee brewing, and the welcome sounds of pans clanging. She was ready for food.

The kitchen buzzed and hummed with activity; it bore an odd resemblance to the reception. Mrs. Wyzenski and Lance were there, Sushi (a drooling George McGovern in his lap), Wanda, Bert, Mo, and a frightened looking Silver cowering in the corner. Jenny blinked in surprise. "Did you all sleep over?" she asked hoarsely. "Did we have an orgy?"

"Have some coffee," Mrs. Wyzenski said firmly. "And eat." She pointed a gnarled old finger to an empty place at the table.

Jenny, glad for once to be following orders, promptly sat. The food was delicious. Lou had baked biscuits for the occasion and Jenny slathered them with huge portions of butter and orange marmalade. She closed her eyes in ecstasy as they slid slowly down her gullet to rest soothingly in her acid-filled stomach. "Aaaahhhh," she sighed. "Aaahh." She ate slowly, one hand cradling her still rocky head.

Once through with breakfast and sitting back comfortably with a scalding cup of coffee, it began to dawn on her that the atmosphere in the kitchen was somewhat tense. Everyone was quiet—an unusual state for her friends. Even Silver refrained from making his usual pedagogical pronouncements. Some were staring at her with a peculiar intensity while others seemed to be avoiding meeting her eyes.

"Did I kill someone last night?" Jenny cracked. "Or screw somebody I shouldn't have?"

Silver transferred his gaze to the ceiling while Sushi seemed to find something quite interesting on the floor. The others either cleared their throats or made coughing noises.

Only Lance seemed unaffected by the general air of constraint. "Why's everyone acting so strange?" he asked, puzzled. "I just think everything's terrific! Couldn't have happened to a nicer person!"

"Shut up," Mrs. Wyzenski hissed.

Lance raised his eyebrows. "Honesty is the best policy, I always say. Let her see it."

"Oh, here," Lou said with a sigh, as she fished a newspaper from the basket on the back of Mrs. Wyzenski's wheelchair. "Haggis devoted his entire column to your exhibit."

"Oh." That was the best Jenny could do.

"Well, take it," Lou said, holding the paper in front of Jenny.

"Why don't you just tell me what it says," Jenny said weakly. "I'm starting to feel sick again."

"Coward." Lou shoved the paper into her hands.

Jenny read.

BAR MAID MAKES IT BIG

Something odd is happening at the Pearce Gallery this
month: an exhibit of paintings by a Tinsel Town barmaid. Yes, a barmaid! The odd thing is that they're
good!

Art —serious art, that is—has heretofore been the pro-
vince of the professional artist, that dedicated, hard-
working, often garret-living psychotic who contributed
so much to the romance of life. Unfortunately, with the
advent of advertising art and other professional outlets,
that breed has disappeared. Today's artists live in pent-
houses on Wilshire Boulevard, drive Ferraris, and have
stock portfolios that could put J. Paul Getty to shame.
But those fair-haired boys, it seems, left more than just
money behind on their many trips to the bank. Their
work has become decorative, pleasant, fun—mere ad-
juncts to interior decoration. Our boys have forgotten
the visions of Hell which once inspired their work.

But then along comes this barmaid—a beautiful, red-
haired nymph who seems to have that vision of Hell all
sewn up.

Her canvasses are nightmares of twisted, distorted
bodies, all screaming at some unseen, unknown horror,
replete with disemboweled corpses and grotesque skel-
etons, flesh hanging in shreds.

These paintings are ugly. This little barmaid chal-
lenges the popular assumption that art exists to hang
over the dining room table.

But, then, how can a true vision of Hell be beautiful?

I'm beginning to think that our artists these days—our
bright, brittle fair-haired boys—have gotten a little too
slick for their own good. Compared to this untrained
talent, their work seems diluted to a hemophiliac level.

Perhaps—to pay for our sins—we need this raw, search-
ing, but very real talent to bring Art (with a capital A)
back to us. Art should be powerful. It should pick us
up out of our Eames chairs and shake some sense into
us.

This beautiful girl's work does.

This redhead's name is Jenny West. Remember it.
You're going to be hearing that name a lot.

And by the way, all you fair-haired boys out there.
Take warning! You know you're slowing down if the
girls are starting to catch up.

Jenny looked up from the paper. The walls were
tilting; another earthquake?

"Jen! Jen!" Lou grabbed her by the arm. "Now
don't get excited!"

"Yeah," said Sushi. "It was a good review, wasn't
it, Lou? Tell her that it was a good review."

"Oh, yes, Sushi. Jenny. It's a good review. A very
good review. *Vision of Hell*—remember?"

"Powerful," quoted Mrs. Wyzenski. "It says your
work is powerful."

Jenny gasped for air. The room seemed so crowded,
so close, so stuffy. She wished Lou would fan the paper
faster.

"Boy," gushed Lance. "Tinsel-town barmaid. That's
really poetic, isn't it?"

Jenny stared at his beaming face and finally got
enough breath to make one pertinent comment.

"FFUUUUUUUUUUUUUCCCKKK!" she screamed.

An hour later she had finally calmed down enough to
speak coherently. "Barmaid! Red-haired nymph! That
motherfucker. *The boys must be slowing down 'cause
the girls are catching up!* Silver—you did this to me
on purpose, you bald-headed prick!"

Lou gasped. "Oh, Jenny. You're wrong!" She threw
a pleading glance at Silver, who looked stricken. "Silver
was just trying to do you a favor. He respects you,
Jenny. He wouldn't do that to you!"

"That son of a bitch doesn't respect God!" Jenny
cried. "He set me up! *Barmaid. Raw. Untrained!*"
Jenny shook her head in disbelief. "Untrained, for
Christ's sake! That bastard just took it for granted that

a woman can't be professional. He never even bothered to check!" Jenny looked around wildly. "Where's that bottle of Scotch?"

Lou looked exhausted. "Oh, Jenny, you're not going to start drinking at ten in the morning, are you?" She saw Jenny's face and then rushed to get the bottle.

Sushi leaned against the stove, dragging on a joint. "Well, old girl, shitty as it is, you've got to admit one thing."

"Yeah, what?" Jenny snarled.

"It sure as hell is going to sell your stuff. I'll bet old Pearce has already jacked up all the prices—and don't forget, you get two-thirds of the bread."

Jenny glared at him as Lou arrived with the bottle. They let her take two swigs then took the bottle away.

Jenny sat glumly for awhile, then sighed and said, "Jesus. What a situation. A long time ago I gave up on people treating me like a person—a human being instead of a stereotype. I wanted to be something other than just a cunt in a crowd. I wanted to be Jenny West. Accepted for what I was. Well, I'm a realist, so I gave up. It's going to be years, centuries maybe, before men can look upon women as people. So why should I beat my head against a brick wall? I decided that I'd just make do with my acceptance as an artist—if that ever came. So now look. After all these years it looks as if I'll finally get the recognition, but I'm not getting it as an artist. I'm just a painting redhead. Still a cunt in a crowd!"

Sushi nodded glumly. "I agree, old girl, I agree. To a certain extent it was done to me, too. Everybody I sell a painting to wants me to spout some Eastern philosophy at them, and shit, I don't even speak Japanese."

Silver agreed. "They do it to everybody, Jenny. The people always have to have their freak. Why do you think I make movies about turds? I hate to admit it, but the mere fact that you're a woman is freak value enough for them."

Jenny sat quietly. Lou poured her another cup of coffee which Jenny left untouched.

After more attempts to cheer her up, Jenny's friends finally left, shaking their heads. Bert said to Mo as they went out the door, "Hell. I'd give my right arm for one-tenth as good a review as McSelfright gave Jenny. I'd learn to paint with my fucking left. But Jen? She wants it all or she doesn't want anything."

Mo patted him on the shoulder and the two walked down the street together.

That night, when Lou and Silver were in bed, Jenny dressed and went out. She walked aimlessly for awhile, then suddenly headed for the Pink Pussy. The juke box was turned full up but she could still hear the laughter from the customers, the shouts of the new waitress. Cigarette smoke drifted out and merged with the smog on Beverly Boulevard.

Jenny stood in the pink glow of the neon sign for awhile, then walked away.

Someone in the cottages had planted lilacs. Their sweetness rose to meet the sour smell of the city. As she passed the cottage where they grew, she reached out and touched the white blossoms. They were covered with black dust.

Then she came to the place her studio had been. There, for an entire block, stretched gray concrete divided by crisp, white lines. In the center stood a little hut with a sign: Carlos' Car Park. Park all day for only $1.75.

She stood shivering in the suddenly cold air. Over the sound of squealing tires and drunken yells she heard a dove mourn. Another answered. Jenny wiped her eyes.

"Hell, old girl," she muttered. "Come off it. You never were a follower of the Romantic School, remember?" She looked up at the moon. It had forced its silver light on the concrete. "Study in Gray, Silver, and White," she mused. "Yes. I could do something with that."

She gave the parking lot one last look and began the long walk back to Lou's.